You Know When the Men Are Gone

**Center Point
Large Print**

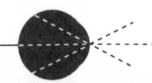

**This Large Print Book carries the
Seal of Approval of N.A.V.H.**

You Know When the Men Are Gone

SIOBHAN FALLON

CENTER POINT LARGE PRINT
THORNDIKE, MAINE

This Center Point Large Print edition is
published in the year 2011 by arrangement with
G. P. Putnam's Sons, a member of
Penguin Group (USA), Inc.

Additional acknowledgments can be found on page 247

The text of this Large Print edition is unabridged.
In other aspects, this book may vary
from the original edition.
Printed in the United States of America.
Set in 16-point Times New Roman type.

ISBN: 978-1-61173-019-7

Library of Congress Cataloging-in-Publication Data

Fallon, Siobhan.
You know when the men are gone / Siobhan Fallon.
p. cm.
ISBN 978-1-61173-019-7 (library binding : alk. paper)
1. Military spouses—Fiction.
  2. Families of military personnel—Fiction.
  3. Large type books. I. Title.
PS3606.A45Y68 2011b
813′6—dc22

2010049387

You Know
When the Men
Are Gone

To KC:

Best friend, husband, father, soldier,

you are always worth the wait.

CONTENTS

She turned to descend the stair, her heart
in tumult. Had she better keep her distance
and question him, her husband? Should she run
up to him, take his hands, kiss him now?

. . . And she, for a long time, sat deathly still
in wonderment—for sometimes as she gazed
she found him—yes, clearly—like her husband,
but sometimes blood and rags were all she saw.

—Penelope upon recognizing Odysseus,
The Odyssey

YOU KNOW
WHEN THE MEN
ARE GONE

In Fort Hood housing, like all army housing, you get used to hearing through the walls. You learn your neighbors' routines: when and if they gargle and brush their teeth; how often they go to the bathroom or shower; whether they snore or cry themselves to sleep. You learn too much. And you learn to move quietly through your own small domain.

You also know when the men are gone. No more boots stomping above, no more football games turned up too high, and, best of all, no more front doors slamming before dawn as they trudge out for their early formation, sneakers on metal stairs, cars starting, shouts to the windows above to throw down their gloves on cold desert mornings. Babies still cry, telephones ring, Saturday morning cartoons screech, but without the men, there is a sense of muted silence, a sense of muted life.

At least things were muted until a new family moved into apartment 12A. Meg Brady from 11A could hear the rip and tear of boxes, chairs

13

scraping against the floor, cabinets opening and closing, the weighed-down tread of the movers reminiscent of the soldiers far away.

Carla Wolenski from 6B knocked on Meg's door around noon, slipping into Meg's living room as soon as she cracked opened the door.

"Natalya Torres is your new neighbor!" Carla whispered, swinging her baby from one hip to the other. When Meg didn't show the enthusiasm or dread Carla expected, she held her baby close as if shielding it from the ignorance of the world. "You haven't heard *anything* about her?"

Meg shook her head. Carla lifted tweezed eyebrows into small parentheses of dismay. She whacked the baby on the back, who promptly burped a milky chunk onto her shoulder. "Trust me, you'll hear it all soon enough," Carla said, flicking the spit-up onto Meg's carpet. When Carla left, Meg followed her out onto the landing, ostensibly to walk her friend back to her own apartment, but she hesitated outside the Torreses' open door, trying to see inside.

The next morning, Meg was woken by a thunderous noise. She reared up, breathless, her heart a wild creature in her chest. Her alarm clock read 5:47 A.M. The noise continued, a mournful, doomed desire, and Meg realized that it was a half howl, half bark, from a dog on the other side of the wall she shared with the Torreses' master bedroom.

14

She slapped her headboard, which made the barking louder, as if the dog were jubilant that he had roused her. She heard him jump, his nails scratching, trying to dig through to her, the otherness of new territory and scent.

Unable to fall back asleep with the foraging a few inches from her pillow, Meg crawled out from her sheets, made a pot of coffee, and checked the Internet for news of Iraq. She scanned the stories about roadside bombs and soldiers dead, making sure the First Cavalry Division and her husband's battalion, 1-7 Cav, were unscathed, at least for today. When the sun rose and the caffeine kicked in, she grabbed her keys and went to the community mailbox on the landing outside, eager for news. She imagined a postcard, like the one Jeremy had sent her a few weeks ago of a flowering Tigris River; she longed for something he had kept in the breast pocket of his uniform, scrawled and hesitated over during a quiet moment while training Iraqi troops. She wanted something she could hold.

A door opened and a black dog bounded out and ran straight at her, a solid bear-rug of muscle. Pizza flyers fluttered to the tile. She closed her eyes and wondered if army doctors would be able to reconstruct her face before Jeremy came home.

"Boris, *down!*" someone shouted just as Meg felt the nails of the dog hit her stomach, knocking the air and any ability to scream out of her. She heard the rattle of a chain and then the dog's weight was lifted. Meg took a half-furious, half-relieved-to-be-alive breath, and opened her eyes. The woman at the other end of the leash was tall and blond, wore an odd patchwork coat that reached to her ankles, its metallic thread catching the early light. She tugged the leash savagely for good measure, muttered, "Down!" again as the dog smiled at Meg, his purple tongue lolling happily from his mouth.

"I am apologize," the woman said, her accent as thick and clunky as the chain around her dog's neck. "Boris, *bad!* Very bad."

Meg felt her cheeks redden as she touched her own shoulder-length brown hair, hoping she'd brushed it before leaving her apartment. She glanced at her sweatpants and slippers. This woman's beauty was an affront, her yellow hair piled up on top of her head, her long neck, glossy red mouth, and the gold and silver squares of material in her coat. She seemed to have stepped out of a Gustav Klimt painting. Who would wear such a coat, a coat made for cocktails and cool autumn nights, while walking a dog? It was barely eight in the morning and April but already the Texas sun had started to burn over the horizon, that thick and sandy wind of Fort Hood flinging its heat around.

"Please refrain from military police," the

16

woman continued over the dog's panting. Meg noticed that the woman's apartment door was open. Two small children peered out of it, both as blondly anemic as their mother. "Boris always have many complaints. My husband would break his heart if Boris gone. Please, I am apologize very much."

"It's all right," Meg said.

"I am Natalya." She held her left hand out, her nails filed into perfect ovals.

Meg wiped her palm on her sweatpants, introduced herself, and they shook.

Boris the Impaler tried to jump her again.

"Meg, you must promise refrain from military police, okay?" Natalya asked, not releasing her hand, her forced smile revealing a row of ever-so-slightly-crooked bottom teeth. "Please promise."

Meg pulled her hand free and glanced back at the children hiding in the shadow of the door. "It's nice to meet you, too, Natalya," she said as calmly as possible, her stomach throbbing from Boris's impact. She left the junk mail on the floor and hurried back to her apartment.

When the fridge was empty except for two cans of Diet Coke and a depleted bag of baby carrots, Meg drove out to the Warrior Way Commissary. She hated grocery shopping, she hated cooking without a man to satiate; the only pleasure in her trip was picking out the food she would send Jeremy in a weekly package—beef jerky, Twizzlers and lollipops, hand wipes and magazines, things that could get crushed, exposed to high temperatures, sit in a box for over a month, and still manage to be consumed by home-desperate soldiers.

She walked the meat aisle, passing her husband's favorites: baby back ribs, pork chops, bacon-wrapped filet mignons. She reached out, touching the cold, bloody meat through the plastic. The raw flesh both horrified and mesmerized, and she wondered if a human being would look the same if packaged by a butcher, the striations of fat, the white bone protruding, the blood thin like water in the folds of the wrap. She wondered if wounds looked like this, purple and livid, but with shrapnel sticking out, dust clinging to the edges, blood in the sand. She quickly put the packaged beef down, telling herself that she would not think such things after Jeremy was home.

But tonight she would get a frozen dinner. A vegetarian one.

As she turned down the next aisle, she noticed a woman rocking her cart back and forth with two children inside. Meg squinted; only one person could have a coat like that.

"Natalya?" she called out.

Natalya stared at her without the faintest

recognition, still pushing the cart back and forth as if she were rocking babies. She looked up at the shelves and said softly, "There is so much, I cannot ever decide."

Meg glanced at Natalya's cart. It was full of potatoes and onions and cabbage. "Are these favorites from your home country?" But Natalya did not nod or even seem to understand. Meg played with her wedding ring and spoke slower. "What do you like to cook?"

Natalya picked up a box of Uncle Ben's rice. "I am not good cook. My mother killed when I was girl. No one teach me."

Meg swallowed her grin and stood absolutely still, all words erased from her mind. "Rice is easy," she finally whispered. "And I could teach you how to cook."

"Yes, rice. With flavor. My English reading is very bad. I do not understand but maybe some have pictures?"

Meg began to look at the boxes of instant rice, handing Spicy Jambalaya and Roasted Chicken to the little boy, who began to shake a box wildly in each fist.

Natalya put one of her long-fingered hands on Meg's wrist and asked abruptly, "May I borrow money?"

Meg stared. This was taboo. If a wife was in need there were rules; you were supposed to call the rear detachment commander and he could approve an official Army Emergency Relief loan. Or, if you didn't want your husband or his command to find out, there were the shifty money shops on Rancier Avenue that let you borrow, at interest, until the next paycheck came through.

"Please," Natalya continued, smiling harder, her lipstick cracking a bit at the sides of her mouth. "Please. Only forty dollars. Very urgency."

Meg looked around to see if she recognized anyone in the aisle, and then, flustered, reached into her purse, pulling out three twenties.

Natalya counted quickly, her cheeks softening at the extra bill.

"Soon I repay, yes?" she said, and immediately pushed her cart away, the boy still shaking the rice. Meg took a deep breath, watching that coat turn a corner and disappear.

Meg looked for Natalya at the Family Readiness Group meeting the following week, the omnipotent "FRG" with its updates from the front, dispelling the fear invoked by CNN with facts and names, always offering ambiguous but hopeful news of return. The FRG Meg belonged to represented 1-7 Cav, an infantry battalion that was exclusively made up of men, which meant that the spouses were all wives. When the husbands were away, the women met regularly and were the closest thing Meg had to a family. It was the closest thing any of them had to family, this simulacrum of friendship, women suddenly thrown together in a time of duress, with no one to depend on but each other, all of them bereft and left behind in this dry expanse of central Texas, walled in by strip malls, chain restaurants, and highways that led to better places. Most of them had gotten used to making a life for themselves without a husband, finding doctors and dentists and playgrounds, filling their cell phone with numbers and their calendars with playdates, and then the husbands would return and the army would toss them all at some other base in the middle of nowhere to begin again.

The wives in Meg's FRG depended on each other for babysitting, barbecue cookouts, pep talks. They brought casseroles when a woman returned to a husbandless house with a newborn, and they remembered each other's birthdays when the men overseas did not. They lived close together on base and they minded each other's business. In a world where it is normal for a thousand men to pack their bags, meet on a parade field, and then disappear for an entire year, the women of deployed soldiers stuck together. Mingling too often with the civilian world, so full of couples, of men nonchalantly paying bills, planning vacations, and picking kids up after ball games, those constant reminders of what life could be, would drive an army spouse crazy.

The FRG leader, Bonnie McCormick, looked every bit the battalion commander's wife: smooth, shoulder-length hair, very little makeup but a perfectly lipsticked smile, conservative blouse with khaki capris, a body that could keep up with the men during their early morning runs.

"Ladies, it is important that you get this information out to the wives who aren't here," Bonnie said, looking around the room. Some wives nodded; most waited to see what was coming next. "You know who they are." She opened the notebook on her lap and began talking about potential return dates for the men, just two months out, and Meg quickly started writing it all down.

Carla leaned into Meg's shoulder and asked, "Did you meet Natalya Torres yet?" Meg nodded, keeping her eyes on Bonnie McCormick. Carla, raising her whispered voice ever so slightly so the wives around them could listen in, continued. "Well, I finally saw her in the laundry room and told her about this meeting but she just shrugged. Her husband's been gone ten months and she hasn't been to one meeting yet." Meg felt something hit her in the neck and looked at Carla's drooling baby, who was waving around a one-pound dumbbell.

"Isn't Mimi strong?" Carla asked, immediately thrusting the baby at Meg. "Whenever I try to take it away she screams bloody murder." Meg would have liked to say, "Please get that Churchill-headed creature away from me," but of course she just took Mimi and jiggled her and made the noises adults make when babies drool all over them. The wives were always throwing their offspring at her as if they thought that the more she got spit up on, the more she'd want one of her own.

"So Sandy from 5C? Her husband used to work with Natalya's in the Green Zone?" Carla spoke with the wonder of an archaeologist newly returned from discovering the eighth ancient wonder of the world. "She told me all sorts of wild things." Meg let Mimi's wet and sticky hand tug on her ear and she gave up trying to take notes. Listening to Carla, she learned that Natalya was Serbian, that she met her husband five years ago when he was stationed in Kosovo and she was cutting hair at his base. He'd been married at the time but quickly divorced the wife who waited patiently for him at home. He brought his new, non-English-speaking bride back to the States when his tour was up.

Bonnie sent a steely glance at the whispering women and they immediately stopped, Meg's cheeks burning as if a priest had caught her giggling during Mass. She didn't reveal that Natalya's mother had been killed when she was young, nor did she mention that she had loaned Natalya money. Keeping secrets made her feel as if she was betraying the wives and she felt sweaty and flushed in the room of women. But Carla, not noticing Meg's discomfort, kept talking, her unearthed treasures would not be silenced. As soon as Bonnie started discussing the different places they could reserve for a welcome home party, Carla told Meg about Natalya's twins, Peter and Lara, three and a half years old. They didn't speak any English, Peter still wore a diaper, and the woman who lived directly above them said sometimes they cried the entire night through. Another wife Meg had never spoken to before tapped her on the shoulder and added that Natalya had already used the "My husband would break his heart if Boris gone" and "Please promise refrain from military police" lines on every single inhabitant in the three-floor apartment building. But for all of their complaining about Boris's apocalyptic bark, none of the wives had contacted the MPs. None of them were willing to make that call, although the reason was not Natalya, nor her twins. No, they would not be responsible for the grief her husband would feel when he came back, having survived the year in Iraq, to a home without a dog. They could not play a role in his disappointment and so they went without sleep, cursed under their breath, banged the ceiling or floor with brooms, and smacked their palms against frail drywall.

• • •

Each day it seemed as if Meg could hear Natalya more and more clearly.

The layout of their apartments mirrored each other exactly, so if Meg was reading in the guest bedroom, she could hear Natalya singing lullabies to her children in their room, usually one that sounded like "London Bridge," but not in English, and all day long Meg's head played the endless refrain, *London Bridge is falling down, falling down, falling down, London Bridge is falling down, my fair lady!* Or, watching TV, she'd hear the murmur of English language tapes from Natalya's living room, the voices like a slow mockery of the dialogue of Meg's Discovery Channel. In bed at night the springs of Natalya's mattress would whine as she tossed and turned. Meg heard so much she began to imagine what Natalya might be cooking, the clothes she chose from her closet, which magazines she flipped through while her microwave popcorn popped. The children rarely made any noise, and when they did it was their singsong gibberish. Meg imagined them listening at their wall, mimicking her motions and laughing at her, and she would jump back and turn up the radio or open the fridge noisily so they wouldn't think she was eavesdropping.

Once or twice a week, Natalya got a call at exactly eleven P.M. These were different from the random calls she got from her husband, when she spoke her slow English, punctuated with "What?" or "Hello? Hello? Are you there?" During her eleven-o'clock calls, she spoke Serbian very loudly, as if on long distance, and she always talked for a full hour. Meg started to look forward to these calls, letting the words lull her to sleep, a welcome distraction. The words were impenetrable and yet so close. She was sure Natalya was revealing her deepest secrets.

Sometimes, after the late-night calls, Natalya wept in her bed, muffling her sobs in a pillow. These noises pried themselves into Meg's dreams and she woke from images of an ice-clogged Danube, sluggish and gray, longing for sun. She wondered if Natalya cried for her husband the way Meg cried for Jeremy, or if she cried for something, or someone, else.

Meg worked at the Craft Realm in downtown Killeen, though she had absolutely no experience with crafts. She did have a B.A. in art history, which seemed to charm the manager. And she liked framing, the silence of it, the exact lines, the unforgiving quality of glass and wood and matting. If the knife slipped, the matting was ruined, and that made every success feel especially deserved. It was absorbing work that helped the days go by while she waited for staticky phone calls, infrequent e-mails, or letters. *I miss our life together*, her husband would write over and over again, and it made Meg think that there were three lives between them: the life he was leading in Iraq, the life she was living alone without him, and the dim fantastical life of them together, a mythical past and future that suddenly had no present.

As she handled baby pictures, high school diplomas, Thomas Kinkade prints, she imagined framing her husband's letters. They were coated with fine dust and words full of desire, as if Jeremy and she were courting again, unused to each other, needing those teenage assurances, hearts doodled on the corners of the page, whispers of undying love. She wanted to trap their moments away from each other under glass and wood, as if in this way the distance could be measured and controlled.

There is a sign at the main gate entrance: WELCOME TO THE GREAT PLACE, FORT HOOD. Its greatness stretches for 340 square miles, from the populated main cantonment of Fort Hood, with its war-themed roads of Battalion Avenue, Hell-on-Wheels, Tank Destroyer, to its vast stretches of pitted firing ranges, the targets wavering with heat in the distance, soldiers slumped beneath the insufficient shade of tent netting, sipping from hot canteens. These ranges are notorious for being halted by cattle. Gates surround Hood, manned by men and women with firearms who check all vehicles and turn away anyone who does not have the proper identification, but Texas law will not banish the cows of neighboring farms from roaming the firing ranges, and soldiers wait hours and hours for the muscled, long-horned beasts to make their way out of the sights of the guns.

Fort Hood, like most army bases, has stern-faced offices with tiny windows, square apartment buildings and barracks with their crooked air conditioners and metal stairways, everything industrial in the ugliest way, with few architectural flourishes or decoration. Different bases might have different building materials, red brick versus gray concrete, depending on the wartime era of their construction, but it's always clear that no matter how much money Congress allotted for the army budget, most of it went into the fighting machines rather than the buildings.

The armories, chow halls, bowling alleys, PXs, dental clinics, libraries, day cares, and schools of Hood are mostly one-story, rectangular creatures of yellowish concrete, and so the taller, glassier buildings, III Corps Headquarters or Darnall Hospital, seem like futuristic and triangular Godzillas standing off at each other. The grass is patchy with tangled cypresses leaching the last of the water from the thirsting earth; the motor pools are picketed by barbed wire; the Burger King and gas station huddle together as the only dabs of color for as far as the eye can see. But when the soldiers deployed, when the eighteen thousand soldiers of the First Cavalry Division went to Iraq, the base shifted from a world dominated by camouflage uniforms to one of brightly colored baby carriages and diaper bags, Mommy & Me meetings at the First Cavalry Museum, women on pastel picnic blankets lounging on the parade field and sharing cinnamon rolls. Though a division of soldiers was far away, the retreat still sounded at five o'clock each evening, blared through speakers across the entire base, and the women stopped their moving cars and got out, stood in the streets with their hands over their hearts, facing the flag just as their husbands would have done, until the bugle's song was over.

Wives with lawns quickly learned to mow them or hire the neighbor's teenage son lest they get a military police citation for letting the grass grow too long. The spouses admired each other's flower beds, the unit crest banners they hung over their name-tagged doors, the small American flags that they pressed into the edges of the driveways, the yellow ribbons they tied around the trees out front. They shopped together, shared leftovers, watched each other's kids so they could go to the gym. They attended church and Bible study, baked brownies and mailed them to soldiers, washed cars to raise money for school supplies for Afghani and Iraqi children.

The women tried to reach out to Natalya, they really did. They invited her to play groups and luncheons and teas, they offered to babysit her children so she could have a break. And all along they were afraid of her. They knew she could happen to any of them. She could be the girl cutting their husbands' hair right now in Baghdad, shipped in from some economically devastated country, young and lovely and for goodness' sake a *woman* in that place of men. Who wouldn't fall in love with such a girl when he was so far from home and so close to death? A woman's soft hands along the short ridge of his hair, on his sunburned neck, holding the mirror up for him to see his reflection next to hers.

But Natalya never accepted any of their invitations. With Boris tugging her wildly, she walked around Hood in that coat you could spot a mile away, her earrings glinting, her lips perfectly painted, making all the other wives assess their figures in the mirror or tug at their shirts self-consciously, touching their hair, rubbing powder into their sweat-shiny faces, knowing it was no use.

This is what they all knew and whispered about Natalya: She didn't bake or make posters, and she never offered to wash a car. She didn't take her children to any of the parks on post. She shopped at the commissary and filled her cart with odd foods, always cabbages and onions and potatoes, sometimes a gallon of chocolate milk or ice cream, but never anything nutritious enough to feed a pair of three-year-olds. She went out a few nights a week, dressed to cause a scandal: high heels, plenty of rouge, earrings long enough to touch her collarbones. She went out alone, and if the wives met her on the stairs and tried to ask where she was headed at ten o'clock at night, she would smile as if she didn't understand the question and continue tottering down to the parking lot below. No one ever saw a babysitter enter her apartment, even though plenty of wives had volunteered, eager to get a look at the interior of her home and refrigerator. They had all seen Natalya lock the door behind her when she went out, and they all imagined those children inside with the television on, alone, the apartment's sharp corners waiting for their soft heads. But no one ever called Family Services. Instead they thought of her husband coming home to discover both children gone.

Meg was spending more and more time alone. She would rush back to the apartment building when her shift finished at Craft Realm, run up the stairs, lock the door behind her. She would take a deep breath, move through her rooms as quietly as possible, and listen.

She listened to Natalya in her kitchen, smelled cabbage simmering through the walls, and heard the scrape of spoon against plate as she fed her children, knife clumsily chopping against a wood board, Boris lapping from his water bowl. Later, she listened for the chime of Natalya's keys, the whine of Boris signaling good-bye, the protest of children who didn't want to go to bed, sharp heels pinging on the steel steps outside. She knew Natalya would be gone for hours. Then Meg would try even harder to hear through those walls, to listen for a child's scream, to be ready to finally call the MPs if need be. More and more often she tried to stay awake with a book until Natalya came home. She listened for the same click of heels, the keys against the front door, the muted thud of shoes kicked off. She always returned very late, usually around two A.M., and Boris yelped with joy that she'd come back to him.

Meg didn't tell Carla about her eavesdropping, though Carla was always asking Meg if she had learned anything new about Natalya. Nor did Meg admit that she was relieved to stay awake listening for her neighbor's children, happy to worry about something other than her husband, or that she fell asleep as soon as Boris finished barking and slept soundly until her alarm went off. Then she was off to work, grateful to have so little time for her own silent thoughts.

One night there was a knock on Meg's door. Natalya stood outside, moving from foot to foot as if her high heels hurt her.

For a moment Meg thought Natalya was going to ask her to go out with her, that they would go to some underground Serbian bar and drink vodka martinis while strange men watched them from the shadows.

Instead Natalya handed Meg three crumpled twenty-dollar bills.

Meg took the money and hesitated, waiting, but Natalya just stared as if she wanted a receipt. She was wearing an orange lipstick that made her cheeks gray. Meg smiled through her disappointment and said softly, "You know, I could watch your children for you. I only work days, and could watch them at night, that way they wouldn't be alone. In case something happened."

The skin of Natalya's pale neck turned red, but Meg couldn't tell if it was from anger or embarrassment.

"A woman must go out sometimes, yes?" Natalya asked softly. "Husbands do not understand. The babies sleep, nothing will happen. It is common in my country—we do not worry so much."

Meg folded the money into a back pocket. "Still. I could watch them."

"Perhaps," Natalya said, lifting her shoulders slightly in annoyed acquiescence. Before Meg could nod in reply, Natalya turned away.

Before Jeremy left, he and Meg had talked about having children. She smiled and blinked and told him, *Soon,* and then ran into the bathroom and checked that she'd taken her birth control pill that day.

She was twenty-eight, it was time to think about procreation, and yet Jeremy's long absences were hard enough to bear without children. She just managed to get through each day, brush her teeth, go to work, feed her body, sleep. If it was almost impossible for her to live half a life without the man who was supposed to share all of it, how could she be both father and mother for some unfinished and needy little being?

There were days when she imagined going to California, a place of escape with its beaches and wineries, mountains and fog. She could get a job in an art gallery in one of those dreamy, gentle-named coastal towns: Monterey, Carmel-by-the-Sea, Big Sur. She'd start over, find a man who was always there, who could take normal vacations, have weekends off, call in sick, accompany her to her cousin's wedding, her uncle's wake. She wanted to worry about ordinary things like whether her husband forgot his lunch or got a bonus, not that he might get shot or that he'd be crossing a street in Baghdad and never get to the other side.

She carried her worry night and day. It pulled at her legs and shoulders and tear ducts, always there and ready to consume her, because how could anyone think rationally about a spouse in a war zone? And when Jeremy, late at night those few weeks before he left, had cupped her body against his, kissing her belly and longing to fill it up with his child, she'd thought only of the worry already growing there. She wondered if her belly could carry a life as well, if there was space for both and if the worry would form a stone pillow for her baby's head. Would it leach into the baby's bones and blood and tiny cells? Now she thought of Natalya and those eerie-eyed twins, whispering a Serbian pidgin in a language only they could understand. Perhaps Natalya nursed a ghostly worry, too. Perhaps her twins remembered another in their mother's womb, three of them waiting to be born.

Meg dreamed of ghost alarm clocks ringing, her husband slipping free of the blanket and letting cold air whisper over her legs, then his kiss by her ear turned into a loud bark. She sat up in her bed and glanced at her clock: 1:23 A.M. Her vigilance had failed her, she had dozed off. She went to get a glass of water and to listen all the better, for she had happened upon a spot in the kitchen wall the size of a fist that another long-ago tenant must have punched and then plastered badly. When Meg put her ear against that papery area, she swore she could hear Natalya breathe.

She quickly stepped backward. A man's voice was audible, just a few inches away, speaking low, as if he had been told to whisper, as if he knew Meg's ear was pressed close. Knives scraped against plates and liquid was poured into glasses. There was a long silence and then Natalya started to speak, almost whimpering. Meg knew there had been no late-night phone calls for two weeks now, and she wondered if this man had been the voice on the phone that moved Natalya to tears. Had he grown tired of the miles between them and appeared at her doorstep after dark, demanding that she let him in?

Footsteps were leaving the kitchen and Natalya's front door opened. Meg looked around her own apartment quickly, grabbed her garbage, and dragged it into the hall, hoping to catch a glimpse of the stranger, but she only saw Natalya in her doorway, her hand pressed to her throat, her face devoid of makeup, as pale as the fluorescent light overhead.

Their eyes met and Meg looked away. Natalya went inside, leaving Meg standing there with her trash.

The man returned, always in the middle of the night. Meg heard food being prepared and drinks poured, but never the noises of consumption. And never—though Meg expected to hear the suspicious sounds of squeaking springs—did they enter Natalya's bedroom.

Still Meg did not confide in the other wives. She imagined asking Bonnie McCormick for advice, pulling her aside and spilling such news into her powerful ear. But she didn't. And she didn't get enough sleep. Natalya was going out more and returning later and Meg fought to stay awake, waiting for Boris's bark, sleeping for a few hours before work. A customer returned a framing job she had done, claiming it was crooked, and her manager, clearly no longer impressed with Meg's degree, said under his breath, "This isn't modern art." And once when she was on the phone with Jeremy, the precious satellite connection full of echoes and clicks, she asked him to hold on while she put her ear to the wall to ascertain if Natalya was still reading her children a bedtime story.

Three days before the men were due back, the wives held a final get-together at Carla's. Each had made six batches of cookies to distribute into care packages for the single-soldier rooms, and almost every wife who lived in post housing was there, perched uncomfortably on one of Carla's overstuffed couches.

"Does anyone know if Natalya is coming?" Carla asked sweetly as soon as Bonnie McCormick entered her living room.

"Natalya Torres, Staff Sergeant Torres's wife?" Bonnie placed her extra-high stack of coconut cookies in the center of Carla's dinner table.

"She lives just down the hall, in 12A," Carla continued, unable to hide her glee. Bonnie stared at the gathered women, waiting for someone to say something, but they all glanced away; none of them had expected Natalya to show and they were scared of Bonnie's straight-toothed smile.

"Well, I'll just run down and knock on her door. Maybe she forgot." Bonnie jingled her bracelets and walked out.

The wives exhaled and then broke into whispers. "Did anyone tell Natalya?" "Yes, I told her when I saw her in the post office last week. She just asked me not to call the MPs on Boris." "I saw her yesterday and she said she was busy but would try to come." "I saw her this morning with that god-awful dog and she let him pee all over the walkway out front—"

Bonnie returned with a plastic plate of cookies in her hand and they all rose in unison. She placed the cookies next to her own on the crowded table and smiled dubiously, not as proud as they expected, which made them gather closer and stare. The cookies were black. Not brown like chocolate or even dark chocolate that was burned. Black like the coal in a naughty child's Christmas stocking.

Bonnie tore open the cellophane and took one, holding it up to the light, her indomitable smile pushed into a frown. "She said these are a Serbian favorite."

They all waited as Bonnie put the cookie under her nose and smelled it, her eyes fluttering in surprise.

Carla took one of the cookies as well, putting it between her teeth with a resounding chomp. Then spit it out into her palm. "It tastes like cabbage," she said.

Bonnie placed her cookie off to the side of the table. "Perhaps Natalya doesn't realize cookies are desserts. Perhaps in Serbia they are meant to be savory?"

"Cabbage!" Carla looked as if she was about to cry, as if someone had tricked her into eating Boris's feces. "We can't put these in the care packages! What if a soldier reaches for one of these"—she threw the cookie on the floor hard where it cracked into tiny scattering pieces— "and thinks *all* of the cookies are bad?"

Bonnie rubbed at her nose as if she could not get the smell of it out of her nostrils. "Some men might like them. Meg, you have the list, are there any single solders with Serbian or Russian last names?"

Meg shook her head without even looking.

"She made us dog biscuits," Carla whispered. Bonnie picked up Natalya's plastic plate and shoved the whole thing into the garbage, and began neatly dividing up the other cookies.

Stunned, the wives joined her, carefully placing assortments of cookies into cheerful buckets, the cookies they had labored over, hoping to arrive with the prettiest shape, the most scrumptious combination, hoping to outdo everyone else with chocolate chips and sprinkles and drizzles of peanut butter and caramel. They did not ooh and aah at each other's works of art the way they usually did. They worked silently, biting their lips, and thought about Natalya.

When Meg returned to her apartment that night, she saw a man silhouetted in front of Natalya's door for a moment, the bright light of the hallway flashing across his sturdy frame. The thickness of his neck frightened Meg, and when she was inside she took down a biography of Chagall, and listened.

She should have tried harder to teach Natalya to cook, she thought. She should have tried.

There were no sounds of strife from next door, just the opening and closing of bureau drawers. At dawn, just before Meg fell asleep, she heard a woman's murmur, thick with tears or laughter, and then, for the first time, the bed creaked on its springs twice as if two bodies slid beneath the sheets, but no noises of lovemaking followed. The next morning Meg woke to absolute peace: Boris must have overslept.

The night before their husbands' arrival, Natalya knocked on Meg's door.

"Please watch children," she said, one long-fingered hand on each child's head. Their matching green eyes peered up.

Meg had been cleaning her apartment and she glanced into her living room, at the pile of unfolded laundry waiting on her couch and the vacuum sitting in the middle of the living room, half of the carpet neatly lined from its sucking groove. It was eight o'clock and Meg was about to say that she couldn't possibly babysit tonight of all nights, she had so much to do before Jeremy returned. But she hesitated, noticing that Natalya wasn't wearing a short skirt and heels, rather a white T-shirt, dark jeans, and flats under her long Klimt coat. Her hair was pulled back into a ponytail and her face was scrubbed clean and pink. For the first time Meg noticed the acne scars on her cheeks and suddenly she understood they had all been wrong. Natalya had been too tall and thin in high school, with bad skin and ill-fitting clothes; other students made fun of her. Natalya had no idea how beautiful she was, which was why she wore that long jacket and rarely left the house without her too-bright lipstick and too-long earrings.

"Of course I will," Meg answered. Natalya nodded, as if it had never occurred to her that Meg would say no, and turned back to her apartment. Meg got her keys, closed her door, and followed.

"They must sleep at nine. Boris already been outside. That is all, yes?"

Meg stepped into the apartment. She was immediately disappointed. No red velvet hung from the walls and no vodka bottles lined the windowsill and shelves; nor did she see sinister posters of Tito or Milosevic. It looked like any of the wives' apartments: light wood table and chairs, fat paperback novels on the bookshelves, a soldier's military awards on the wall, a few primary-colored children's toys scattered on the floor. There was no hint that Natalya was anything but American except for a stack of fashion magazines on the coffee table with Cyrillic writing on the covers, as if she had wiped every shred of her past life away, everything but this one last comfort of elusive beauty.

Natalya got down on her knees and spoke Serbian to her children.

"They will be good," she said when she stood. She turned to Meg. It was hard to take her stare, as if all of the makeup and jewelry in the past had been a filter and now Meg was looking directly at the sun.

"Thank you," Natalya said, her accent making the words sound impossibly grave.

"When will you be home?" Meg asked. The troops were arriving at the First Cavalry parade ground the following day at ten and she wanted to be rested and ready.

"Soon." Natalya kissed each child on the mouth, patted Boris's square head, picked up her small beaded purse, and walked out, leaving her noisy keys behind.

Her children were every bit as good as she had promised they would be, playing quietly with a set of wooden blocks, then going to bed as soon as Meg led them to their room.

Of course Meg crept all around the apartment, especially in Natalya's bedroom. The bed was perfectly made, the walls a somber green, the bedspread a shocking white. There were no family photos on the walls or bureaus, none of Natalya holding twin infants at a hospital, no wedding photos, and no scenes of Serbia. A luminous icon of Jesus, His beard as black as His wet eyes, hung directly over the bed. Meg thought of Natalya in this dark-walled room and understood why she would resist bringing her nightly visitor here. But he had been here the night before, hadn't he? He had finally wormed his way into Natalya's bed. Meg peered at the pale comforter, looking for something sordid, the lacy edge of see-through panties perhaps, and she wondered why Natalya could not have waited just a little bit longer for her husband to come home. Then Meg went out to the living room, turned on the TV, and thought of Natalya's husband, how, like all the others, he was sitting on a plane right now, so excited to return to the States, to his home, to his family. The wives had ensured that his dog and his children had not been taken from him, but Meg knew that his wife had. She knew he would not be returning to a happy home.

Leaning back into the pillows, Meg kicked off her shoes. Soon she wouldn't need to worry about Natalya. Tomorrow Jeremy would be home. That interminable waiting, waiting, waiting for her life to continue—such a long, gray nothingness between departure and return, huge chunks of existence she filled up and pushed through as if it were a task rather than a stretch of her young life—would be over. There was such unreality to the waiting, such limbo; sometimes she didn't even know what she was waiting for. So much wasted time. Time was the enemy, waking her up alone at night and ticking so slowly, each minute mocking her. But now it was over. Jeremy would be back tomorrow and her life would resume and she would no longer care what Natalya did within these walls.

Boris woke her as usual. But this time it was his snout pressing up against her shoulder rather than his bark. It took Meg a moment to realize where she was, that she was stretched out uncomfortably on Natalya's couch. She sat up so quickly that she nearly fell off the cushions, her elbow knocking over the foreign fashion magazines on the table, splaying bare arms, thighs, and lipsticked mouths across the carpet.

Daylight filtered in through the shaded window, Boris was trying to lick her face, and Natalya had never come home.

Meg rose, pushing the dog away, feeling her stomach shift with uneasiness. It was seven in the morning; she told herself that there was still time for Natalya to walk in, for the day to right itself. She creaked open the door to the twins' room. Peter had crawled out of his bed and into his sister's, their small bodies pressed together as if still curved in a womb. Meg closed the door, got Boris's leash from the hook by the door, and took him outside.

He pulled her up and down Battalion Avenue, trying to run into traffic, looking back at her as if he were having an amazing amount of fun. Then he squatted on the perfectly manicured lawn of the Relocation Center and would not move no matter how much she tugged his leash or begged. She hadn't brought a plastic bag to pick up after him, so she covered his mess with leaves, not making eye contact with an old woman who watched from a park bench.

She returned to the apartment, quickly slipping inside. The twins were both sitting up, blinking. They didn't seem surprised to see Meg rather than their mother, and they didn't cry.

Meg changed Peter's diaper, his green eyes watching her stoically as she covered him with baby powder from his thighs to his ribs. Then Lara led Meg by the hand to the bathroom and pointed at the toilet, and did not let go until Meg clapped her hands in praise at the contents. It was eight o'clock in the morning and Natalya had not returned.

Meg held a child on each hip as she made her way to the First Cavalry parade grounds, the greenest stretch of grass on all of Fort Hood. Carla spotted her and rose from her seat high up in the bleachers, almost dropping Mimi in shock. Meg nodded at her friend and squeezed onto a bench in the front, sitting next to a man who wore a baseball cap stitched with *Veteran of Foreign Wars*. He leaned over and gave Lara and Peter small American flags to wave, and Peter immediately shook his flag as if he were trying to separate the stick from the cloth. The Horse Calvary Detachment was beginning its show, soldiers dressed in Custer-era uniforms riding in perfect figure eights across the parade field, their sabers and spurs glinting in the harsh Texas sun. Behind them, a long line of blue buses pulled up on Battalion Avenue.

"Here they come," the vet said, pointing at the buses. "Bet you are excited to see their daddy."

Meg nodded. She had no idea what their father would say, or what she would answer. The sleek horses on the field lined up at one end. A howitzer cannon erupted and the horses charged across, their riders shooting their rifles into the air. The crowd surged to its feet, stamping, clapping, and shouting, and Peter screamed at the uproar, dropping his flag. "Mama," he sobbed, putting his hands to his ears.

"Shhh," Meg whispered, trying to bounce the children. Behind the smoke of the cannon and guns, the soldiers were beginning to exit their buses and line up in formation, their feet slightly apart, their backs so straight, their eyes scanning the crowd for a face that loved them. Meg searched the miraculously appearing men for her husband. "Shhh." Then Lara started to cry, too.

"London Bridge is falling down," Meg began to sing, *"falling down, falling down. London Bridge is falling down, my fair lady!"*

Lara glanced up at Meg's face, recognizing the song. Meg knew there were other stanzas about gold and silver, about locking people up, the destruction and rebuilding of the bridge over and over again, but wasn't it still standing today? It had been toppled by fires and wars, and each time it was resurrected with sturdier stuff. Then Lara began to join in, letting loose a jumble of mysterious syllables, and Peter, his eyelashes clotted with tears, started to softly mumble along.

Meg, repeating the little she knew of the song over and over again, turned toward the men. She had no idea what their father looked like; would he spot his children, who had grown and changed during the year he'd been deployed? Would he recognize them sitting on a stranger's lap? He would be looking for his wife, for her clear blond hair, her patchwork coat, her thin hands. Meg thought of Natalya raising these children alone, Boris bolting and barking and scratching on the door all day, how the twelve months must have been so long in a place where she couldn't even read the directions for instant rice. And so Natalya had gone searching for a man to get her out of the uncertainty of it all, perhaps the way she had searched for a man to get her out of Kosovo. Searched for someone who would always be there, who could take care of her and hold her when she cried at night for the lives she left behind. Natalya had escaped one war and found herself caught in the wake of another; perhaps she realized she could survive without her children but she couldn't take the waiting anymore.

And then Meg saw Jeremy cross through the smoke.

She put the children on the grass, holding their tiny palms, their fingers tight on her knuckles.

Jeremy lined up with all the other soldiers and he immediately found his wife, his eyes locking onto hers. He didn't even glance at the children, just stared at Meg as if she were the anchor that held his life. And Meg did not hesitate. She stood and took a step toward him, knowing suddenly and without a doubt that he was, and always would be, worth the wait.

CAMP LIBERTY

David Mogeson didn't like to tell people about his life before the army, how he had been an investment banker. The words sounded ridiculous to him and therefore he assumed they sounded ridiculous to anyone else. There were the lifted eyebrows, the incredulous laugh—women in bars who thought he was trying to get them into bed or men who thought he was boasting about a mythical life that could never be lived on a soldier's salary. But he wasn't the only one who had joined up after September 11, who threw away a stable, ordinary American life of freedom and money, stirred by waving flags and the elusive vocabulary of an older generation: duty, honor, country. The others who enlisted for the same reasons were easy to spot: they were older and smarter than their rank said they should be and lately they were more cynical than their army peers. They tended to stick together although they didn't talk about their previous lives with one another either. Civilians thought they were patriots but they understood that they were just more naïve than the rest of the country; they had heeded a call that most had not, and now they bided their time, waiting to get out. They told themselves they would tell their war stories to their kids, their grandkids, and then it would all be worth it.

His parents called him David. His friends from Stuyvesant High School, NYU, and Wells Fargo called him David. His girlfriend of four years, Marissa, called him David or a singsong *Dav-vy* when she was angry with him. But everyone in the army called him Moge. And in the couple of years since basic training, "Moge" had become his identity in a way that unnerved him. Suddenly the name "David" felt too refined and prissy in comparison. Too weak. He wanted out of the army before he became this Moge character forever.

He started looking up grad schools from the communal computer room of Camp Liberty, his forward operating base outside of Baghdad. He had seven months, three weeks, and six days of his commitment left—once he got back to Fort Hood, he'd out-process and be back in New York in no time, a civilian again, a student, free.

Then they promoted him to sergeant, even though he had resisted the pressure to reenlist for another year with its twenty-thousand-dollar tax-free reenlistment bonus. A week later his squad leader, Sergeant Raines, was shot through the face, a miracle, missing his eye and nose and somehow even his brain, the bullet emerging through the planes of his face in such a way that Raines kept giving orders during the firefight, had just assumed he'd been fragged in the cheek by wayward shrapnel, until the blood leaking from the back of his neck wouldn't stop and the medic stuck his finger inside and realized it was an exit wound. So Raines was sent to the hospital in Germany and Sergeant Moge, by default, became the acting squad leader. The guys he bunked with, shared *Playboy* magazines with, stayed up all night playing *Call of Duty* with, were suddenly "his men" rather than his buddies. It was the first bit of power the army handed over and it made the Moge in him blossom. While others dragged their feet when they were sent out beyond the wire, Moge's men were ready and yodeling as they climbed into their Humvees, and Moge, though raised in the East Village, began to speak in an inexplicable Queens accent, his use of the word *fuck* explosively poetic.

Just when Moge had become everything the army needed him to be, his favorite interpreter, Khaled, quit. Khaled was getting married and his wife's family thought his job a much too dangerous profession. They did not approve of his having to move to a different relative's house every few days, leaving at dawn and taking many different buses, always a different route to the base in order to avoid being followed.

Khaled apologized profusely, taking Moge's palm in his, staring at him intently and holding his hand much too long in a way that a straight man would never hold another straight man's hand in the U.S.

"She is my first wife," Khaled said. "I am a fool for love."

Moge tried not to smile, but he did manage to turn the hand-squeeze into a handshake, and then carefully remove his fingers from Khaled's grip, patting the man on the shoulder. Khaled's colloquial idiosyncrasies made him the company's most requested terp, not because of his English accuracy but because he had them laughing as they rolled out.

"Congratulations," Moge said, giving Khaled a box with a lopsided bow. He had had Marissa send him a serving platter as a wedding gift. He didn't know if Khaled or his new wife would ever use it, the bottom was stamped with *Made in America* and therefore might be a liability in their home, but Moge had wanted to give him something.

Khaled bowed his head. "Thank you, my cherished friend." He reached for Moge's hand again and Moge did not pull it away.

The army gave him a new terp. A woman terp. Moge was not happy when the first sergeant informed him.

"I thought this was an infantry company, First Sergeant," he said. "And there's a reason we don't have women in the infantry."

First Sergeant looked up from his desk and Moge saw himself through the eyes of the highest-ranking noncommissioned officer in the company—his hair touching his ears, his wrinkled uniform, his lowly rank. Moge waited for the lecture.

"You are here to help this country, isn't that right, Moge?"

Moge bit the inside of his cheek and just barely nodded his head.

"You're not helping anyone if you are cowboying around without an interpreter. Now you have an interpreter. Enough said."

Moge rolled back and forth in his boots, knowing he was dismissed but unable to leave. "What if she . . . I don't know, gets hurt, First Sergeant? The guys are going to worry about a woman in the heat of it. It'll interfere with our mission."

First Sergeant arranged the papers on his desk. "She chose this job. She knows the danger better than any of us."

Just as Moge was about to step out of the office, the first sergeant called him back. "Sergeant, you've really squared away your squad in the last few weeks."

Moge nodded. He remembered how, a couple

of months before, one of the privates was late for company PT, so the entire squad was tasked with building a pathway to the filthy porta-shitters that were cleaned once a month. Six highly trained United States Army soldiers, among them an investment banker, a high school history teacher, and a cop, laying down gravel and scrap wood across a stench-filled morass of sucking mud. Since Moge had taken over, no one had ever been late for PT—hell, their PT scores were the highest in the battalion.

The first sergeant was watching Moge as if he could read his thoughts through his forehead. "Your platoon sergeant says you're thinking of getting out," he said. "Can't imagine why a fast-tracking soldier such as yourself would do that when the civilian job market is headed the wrong way down a one-way." Moge shrugged ever so slightly, enough to voice his disagreement without being outright disrespectful. "Moge, how else you gonna have an opportunity to be a goddamned hero?"

Moge said nothing. When the first sergeant looked back down at his paperwork, disgusted, he turned and walked out.

The new interpreter's name was Raneen. She showed up at formation the following morning wearing camouflage, U.S. Army issue, but the decade-older version, the version used in Desert

Storm, not the ACUs everyone was wearing now. She was small, five feet two inches or so, and seemed even smaller in her loose uniform, the sleeves rolled up a few times at her wrists. Her dark hair was uncovered and pulled back severely into an intricate bun at the nape of her neck. She didn't wear any makeup and her fingernails were unpolished but clean and filed straight across. Moge's men were silent; they had been in Iraq for more than five months and had seen very few women's faces, just shadowy *abayaas* floating like dark, nunnish ghosts down the streets of Baghdad, the occasional American female reporter in a bulky Kevlar vest and surrounded by security, sometimes an older Iraqi woman with a colorful *hijab* scarf over her head in the Green Zone.

Their first mission with Raneen was an easy one: there was a new girls' school on the outskirts of Dora. The headmistress had written a halting letter to the base's battalion commander asking for school supplies and a generator. Moge and his men had a few boxes of pencils and crayons, spiral notebooks and soccer balls, a case of water bottles, six cans of peanut butter, saltine crackers, and apples stolen from the mess hall— if a school was overtly asking for aid from the Americans, it had to be in desperate need.

It was quiet in Moge's Humvee, none of

Khaled's incessant questions about why Americans prefer college football to soccer, why Britney Spears was viewed as more beautiful than the resplendent Catherine Zeta-Jones, why Americans look so fat on television but the soldiers were so skinny.

"Hey, sister!" one of the men shouted from the back of the truck. Moge looked down the line, catching Specialist Brodis Dupont elbow Crawford.

"Welcome to the Boom Boom Room," Dupont continued. Trapped laughter hissed from behind the hands of the soldiers next to him.

"That's 'Boom Boom' Dupont," Moge said to Raneen. "He's survived three IEDs, two of them in this same Humvee." Moge tapped the soft wall for emphasis. "He's first platoon's very own living, breathing lucky charm."

The soldiers high-fived and then Dupont, never one to let the attention of a woman pass him by, called out again, "Lady, maybe you can settle something we've been debating since we got to this upstanding country." He hesitated theatrically. "Do you all eat pork?"

"Cut it out," Moge said. Dupont was a good soldier and a bright kid, had been a third-string tight end at LSU until he ran out of money, blasted gangsta rap through his headphones but smeared sunblock on his cherrywood-dark skin every morning, and called his momma in Baton Rouge once a week. Moge suspected he also had some serious PTSD, that he was the kind of guy who would have a difficult time staying out of trouble back at home when there wasn't a sergeant looking over his shoulder all the time.

"What, Sar'nt? I'm just trying to broaden our 'Moos-lim' cultural awareness. Everybody wants to know if a Muslim can eat hot dogs but nobody asks. Has she ever had the distinct pleasure of biting into a plump, dirty-water dog on a hot summer day? Or maybe a spicy, thick hunk of good ol' Louisiana *andouille* sausage? This is something we are very eager to know." All the soldiers were laughing by now, heads lowered into the stiff padding of their Kevlar vests, their rifles knocking into their helmets, leaning into one another and shaking their heads.

Raneen had been looking out a window but now she slowly turned and directed her gaze at Dupont. She didn't say anything, just stared, the laughter drying up, the men glancing away, until even Dupont lost his grin, finally shrugged, and bent over to tie the already perfectly tied lace of his boot.

Moge rubbed his chin against his shoulder to hide a smile. So this chick might be okay, he thought. Raneen went back to looking out the dust-spattered window, her face emotionless.

Two of the Humvees pulled security around the school, guns out, creating a half-moon of camouflage against the dilapidated building. It had been hit by a mortar to the left of the entrance, the concrete still crumbled and loose, but someone had stuck fake flowers into the rubble and it almost looked cheerful. A tall woman in a head-scarf stood in the doorway wringing her hands, glancing around at the Humvees and soldiers with their guns, looking at the blank windows of the buildings surrounding the school.

The woman spoke to Raneen and Raneen nodded, then whispered to Moge, "She says so many soldiers will bring unwelcome attention."

Moge glanced around, noticing how quiet the streets were. "This is a dangerous neighborhood, ma'am, but we'll be out of here in a few minutes. Dupont!"

Dupont, covered in a sheen of sweat and grimacing, carried three boxes stacked on top of one another. Moge had tasked him with the job of handing out the school supplies to help his quest for "Muslim cultural awareness."

There were no desks in the classroom and the only light came from the windows and the hole in the ceiling left behind by the mortar attack. About twenty young girls in tattered but brightly colored dresses were sitting on the floor, eyes wide, hands folded in their laps. Dupont dropped the boxes, pulled out his knife, and slit them open, the cardboard emitting a low scream. When he started handing out the notebooks and

Crayola crayons, the girls could sit still no longer and got to their feet like skittish does, hiding behind one another but pushing closer to Dupont and his magic boxes, their hands reaching out thin and spindly for his gifts. After securing a book and a pencil or crayon, the children ran into the corners of the room and flopped back down on the ground, opening up the fresh pages of paper and writing on them, tiny letters or shapes so as not to take up too much room, to make the paper last.

"Do you mind giving us a tour?" Moge asked the headmistress, the lines of her face softer now, her hands patting the heads of the children around her. Raneen translated and the woman nodded and led the way.

There were two other rooms. One had stacks of thin blankets folded against the wall, the other small wooden cupboards and a rusty sink that clearly had not produced water in a long while. He was glad that they had managed to bring the peanut butter and apples, and before he left he would have the men open up their MRE lunches and hand out the food to the kids. He had seen only a small cracked blackboard but no books and he looked at the headmistress again, wondering if she was the only teacher. Raneen and the woman spoke in whispers and Moge did not mind that she didn't translate every exchange for him; he trusted his terps enough to realize they always told him what he needed to know.

Moge heard a shout from outside and ran to the window. The soldiers, their guns slung across their bulky, Kevlar-shielded backs, had dumped out the box of soccer balls and were kicking them around, and the girls, barefoot and holding their long dresses up to their knees, started kicking them back.

He sat in front of Raneen on the return ride to the base.

She leaned forward in her seat and asked him, "Will the battalion commander approve the generator?"

"I'll write up a report; I'll even talk to the company commander myself."

"The little girls, they sleep there, you know," she continued. "Their parents have sent them from very far away. There is no wash closet or running water but the headmistress, she finds ways to feed them."

She looked to see if anyone was listening but the guys were all intently looking out the windows, the streets still eerie and empty. Moge knew that it was beginning to dawn on them that, while they had been kicking around soccer balls and drawing pictures of American screaming eagles in the little girls' notebooks, insurgents had had plenty of time to plant improvised explosive devices in every roadside pothole or pile of rubbish all the way back to the base.

Raneen continued, "She told me there is a factory one half of a mile east, that it is rumored to have many foreigners working there. She was not explicit but I assume it is where IEDs are perhaps created."

Moge straightened in his seat, lowering his voice. "Are you kidding? How did you manage to get that kind of information?"

Raneen blinked at him. "It is the information we were meant to get. Of course that is why your battalion commander sent us to a girls' school so far away. Dora, as you said, is a bad neighborhood. The headmistress understands that in order to get a generator she must have very good information. You must know that also." She turned her face away as if insulted by Moge's ignorance. Her voice continued, so softly that Moge had to lean closer. "No one notices the women in this country, and therefore no one notices how much the women notice."

Dupont slammed his tray down next to Moge's in the chow hall, his freedom fries sliding across the table.

"Boom Boom." Moge moved his elbow so Dupont could sit down. He could never say the nickname without cracking a smile.

"Sar'nt." Dupont took a few bites of his

hamburger and Moge could feel Dupont's brown eyes boring a hole through his cheekbone.

"What?"

Dupont swallowed, then gulped down half his Gatorade. "I appreciate doing the humanitarian crap and all, but now that we have a woman terp, are we going to get tasked with all the pussy missions?"

Moge sipped his soda, thought of the IED factory that Raneen was now briefing the battalion commander and some Special Forces guys about. "You're not tired of getting blown up?"

Dupont looked down at his food, pushed his fries around in a red sea of ketchup. "It's because I got blown up that I want to shoot the shit out of the bad guys." He spoke as if he had practiced the line, and Moge wondered if Dupont was writing his own rap and broadcasting himself on YouTube.

"Patience, Dupont. We probably did more for the war giving those girls notebooks than any other mission in the past five months."

"You know"—Dupont drawled his words in a swift change of mood—"that new terp is kind of hot, if you like the stuck-up schoolteacher type."

Moge laughed and stood.

Dupont flashed his easy, college-athlete "Ain't I something?" smile. "The last woman terp, that skinny-ass one working with Blackthorn? She got hitched to a Swedish contractor. Y'all let 'em walk around without a burka and they don't ever want to go back to the imams. Watch out, Sarg, you might be next."

Moge lifted his tray. "Just don't let me hear you asking any more questions about pork."

Moge went home to New York for his two weeks of mid-tour leave. His parents had moved out of the city soon after 9/11, to a house on the outskirts of Cold Spring, a small town north of Manhattan, near the Hudson River and commuter trains. Marissa came to visit, carrying a huge suitcase twice the size of Moge's duffel bag, wearing a short wool skirt and high-heeled boots. Her parents and Moge's had been friends for decades; they used to share a house together in the Hamptons in the summer, where Moge would make fun of Marissa's braces until she cried, and now his parents had a guest room done up in lavender that they called "Marissa's room."

His mother sent them out before dinner for wine and French bread. Moge drove his father's BMW too fast, his eyes everywhere, looking for abnormalities on the side of the road that might be hiding an IED, waiting for a truck to come careening into him. Marissa tried to laugh from the passenger seat, holding on to her seat belt.

The grocery store was overwhelming, the shelves high, so many colors and options, the lights too bright. Marissa slipped her arm through his and led him to the cereal aisle, boxes of primary-colored cereal rising from floor to ceiling, accosting him with leering cartoon characters and flavors painted to look like they were exploding from bowls of milk.

"Are Trix still your favorite?" she asked, as if it was a private joke between them, but Moge just shrugged.

He could smell her flowery perfume, probably something ridiculously expensive and advertised by a rock star. He knew he'd been cold toward her; he had not yet told her how beautiful she was, that he liked the new highlights in her hair, that he was happy she had come upstate to see him. "Get whatever you like," he said. "I can eat anything."

She blinked and then reached for the Trix anyway, putting the box in the basket next to the California Zin and still-warm loaf of French bread.

As they left the aisle, Moge heard a tall woman speaking to a young man in a red grocery vest, "—how many times do I have to ask for Organic Fresh O's? It's the only cereal my Ashley will eat. I have been shopping here faithfully for five years—"

Moge stopped and stared at the woman in her

cobalt blue horn-rimmed glasses. He thought of the barefoot girls in the Dora school and he suddenly wanted to punch this woman in the head.

"Dav-vy!" Marissa called from the end of the aisle. The woman in the glasses had stopped speaking and was watching Moge, her plucked eyebrows lifted with annoyance and perhaps fear at the way he was standing too close. Moge turned and followed Marissa's boots to the cashier.

He had a runny nose and he was tired all the time. He told his family it was jet lag and he tried to stay in bed even when he heard Marissa's voice outside his bedroom door each morning, offering him coffee and pancakes.

His father asked him if he wanted to go down to the city one day, to the Diamond District, perhaps? And Moge had coughed behind his hand. So they all thought he was about to propose, or that he *should* propose, which would explain why his parents kept sending him and Marissa out each night to a different restaurant, and Marissa's red-rimmed eyes each morning when he had not. They had had sex only twice during the last week, when his parents were out golfing, and it had been fast and unsatisfying, Marissa stunned and silent on his childhood bed when he was done. She was leaving in two days, home to Long Island and her second-grade class, and Moge was glad.

He wanted to be back in Baghdad. The platoon leader was new and Moge worried about his men. It was a pain in the ass to find a different route back to base each day with the roads blocked off, covered in shit and rubble, and he knew his men would get complacent. Would the young lieutenant remember to rearrange the order of the Humvees so that the insurgents didn't know where the leadership was situated in the convoy, especially with his satellite "bat wing" antenna sticking out his passenger window like a big bull's-eye? Would the LT know to stay away from the corner of Yarmouk, near the marketplace, where IEDs seemed to always go off no matter how many times they barricaded and searched the street? What about the overpass on Route Tampa where Jaish al-Medi dumped the bodies of the people they had tortured and killed? Did the lieutenant know that they had also started placing bombs under the corpses, hoping to kill the American or Iraqi soldiers who gathered them up and brought them to the morgue?

Everything at home annoyed him and he knew it was irrational and misplaced, but did Marissa really need to watch *Extra!* every night to catch up on Jessica Simpson's latest breakup? Did one missing woman in Missouri—sure, she was pretty, a wife and the mother of three—really need to be the headlining story on every single news program when there were American soldiers, mothers and fathers, wives and husbands, dying in Iraq and Afghanistan? Why weren't Larry King and Barbara Walters interviewing their grieving families or telling their intricate life stories?

He tried, he really did, he tried to care when Marissa told him about her second-graders with their video games and peanut allergies, or when his mother complained about gas prices, or when his father had a lousy day of golf. Something was wrong with him, some part of him was still keyed into Baghdad, into his Humvee, his night-vision goggles, his men riding down streets not knowing what was at the end of them, and everything that he thought would make him happy here at home suddenly seemed so inconsequential. He couldn't even go for a run anymore on old 9W—past the stone Episcopal church with its early-nineteenth-century cemetery, the governor's white house half hidden by shady trees, down to the Garrison train tracks to glimpse the Bear Mountain Bridge sparkling over the water, the route he always took when he visited his parents—because one of their neighbors, an obese, fifty-five-year-old banker in a Yankees cap, might be riding his mower, *riding a mower* for a quarter-of-an-acre plot of water-sprinkled and coiffed Technicolor-green grass, and every time Moge saw his smug, fat face he wanted to jump over the guy's white picket fence and beat the living shit out of him.

He had to get back to Baghdad soon.

Of course, when he did get back, he told everybody what they wanted to hear. That the food had never been better, filet mignon and fried calamari that melted in his mouth, beer so cold it stung his tongue, gin tonics and vodka martinis and screwing his girlfriend at least three times a day.

His runny nose immediately dried up and he felt alert again, awake at dawn to the call to prayer that reverberated around the base. It was as if his body had grown dependent on the 120-degree days and the 40-degree nights, the long-sleeved camouflage uniform and the heavy lace-up boots, the weight of the helmet and the forty-pound Kevlar vest, the tinny water fed into his mouth by a warm tube from the CamelBak slung over his shoulder, the churned-out high-calorie but tasteless eggs at the chow hall in the morning, the dried-out MRE bagged meals in the afternoon, sleep-deprived nights of helicopters landing or mortars ringing with the usual bad aim against the perimeter of the base. His body thrived in the desert; his Moge thrived while the weak little David crawled deeper into hibernation. And Moge was seized with a terrible thought: What if, after all of his longing to get out and get on with his life, in his comfortable middle age he would look back at this time and realize that his years in the army were the most vivid, the most startlingly real, of his entire life?

Maybe he should not be getting out after all.

Raneen smiled when she saw him, the first time he had ever seen her teeth, small and white but slightly crooked in front; she suddenly looked like a kid with those funny front teeth, and it made something in his stomach go soft.

"Did I miss anything?" he asked, squinting into the sun.

"The girls' school received a generator," she replied. Moge had overheard the first sergeant and company commander bitching about the Rangers and Special Forces guys coming in and taking over one of their high-value targets and he wondered if maybe the Dora IED factory had been it.

"Good work," he said, and Raneen blushed a high red over her sharp cheekbones. Moge had to look at the sun again, letting it blind him for a moment so he wouldn't blush, too.

Their next mission was not a humanitarian effort in any way. Their battalion had been relying on an informant for the past few months,

Yasin Mustafa, a rich merchant who had a concrete compound and armed bodyguards. He had helped them catch a few members of Jaish al-Medi, but recently Mustafa's information had brought the battalion under sniper fire. The first time the battalion commander thought Jaish al-Medi had been lucky, that they just happened to have a sniper in the building across the street, but when it happened again and an American soldier died during a raid, they knew that Mustafa was no longer trustworthy. So Moge and a platoon of Iraqi soldiers were going into Mustafa's compound in the middle of the night to bring him back to the base for questioning.

Raneen sat steely-faced in the Humvee; she usually didn't do the night missions and Moge wished that another terp had been chosen. But Mustafa had four wives and many children and Raneen would talk to them, would perhaps find out in a few hours what military intelligence would never find out from Mustafa.

There were no shots fired. The bodyguards shouted and waved their AKs but when they saw how outnumbered they were, they suddenly shrugged and smiled and started sharing cigarettes with the Iraqi soldiers who accompanied the Americans. Mustafa himself came out with his arms open and invited everyone in for tea and dates, and agreed, with only a slight narrowing of his eyes, to return to the base.

"I bring a lawyer, yes? Like on American television. Miranda rights?" And he laughed with such confidence that Moge knew he would be free by morning no matter how many U.S. soldiers may have died because of his double dealing. They didn't even need to cuff him.

Raneen emerged from his house a few minutes later, her face tilted down, and Moge assumed she hadn't had any luck either. The ride back was quiet, none of the usual high fives and whoops of delight from a mission accomplished, as if every soldier knew that tonight had been a waste of time, that they may have gotten the bad guy, but in the end the bad guy had gotten one over on them.

"So the women didn't give anything up?" Moge asked Raneen.

She turned toward him, her eyes full of pupil and fear. "His second wife said she knew me," she whispered. "That I am an infidel and will die an infidel's death."

Moge tried to smile. "I hear that all the time."

Raneen shook her head. "She knew I am a widow. That my husband was a professor. She knew me."

Moge wiped sweat from his face—he didn't know Raneen was a widow. "Maybe you ought to live on Camp Liberty for a while; you'd be safe and could even sleep in in the morning."

But she looked away. "I have a daughter."

Moge swallowed—he didn't know that either. He had assumed Raneen was in her twenties but now in the dim light from the Humvee controls she looked older, early thirties, perhaps, with lines around her mouth.

"Maybe just for a little while," he said. "I don't think there are any other women terps right now so you'd get your own quarters. You could visit your daughter on your days off."

Raneen nodded, tears in her eyes, and Moge looked away in embarrassment. This is why there aren't any women in the infantry, he thought to himself, but his stomach went soft again and he was relieved that Raneen would be close by.

Moge's once-weekly calls to Marissa became more haphazard. He started thinking that maybe she was too young for him. She was only twenty-four to Moge's twenty-nine years, which had always seemed like a bonus: if she was younger she'd be less likely to want to get married anytime soon; her friends were single and she still took trips with them to Cancún or Las Vegas; she seemed content to live at home with her parents and never even asked if she and Moge should move in together; and her maternal clock, as much as she loved her students, had yet to kick in. But suddenly Moge thought she was too childish, too vain, too blond, and there were long silences during their conversations. He was glad when the static became thick enough for him to hang up without having to say, *I love you.*

"Hey," he said, spotting Raneen at a corner table of the mess hall one night just as he was leaving. He stood holding his dirty tray, uncertain if he should move on. She grinned up at him and nudged her tray so there was room for him to sit.

"I have been wanting to tell you of my gratitude," she said. She crossed her hands primly in front of her and Moge thought how right Dupont had been when he called her a schoolteacher. "Staying on base has been a very good idea."

Moge felt the eyes of soldiers glancing off of him and he fiddled with his empty cup of 7UP. "That's great."

She leaned toward him. "It is how I imagine an American university to be. When we interpreters get back late and are not tired, we play checkers or dominoes and tell stories. Of course I worry about my daughter, but it is very free to not be frightened every morning and every evening, traveling to my home, worrying someone will follow and murder myself and my family. Even with the helicopters I sleep very soundly. I am thankful to you, Sergeant Mogeson."

He squirmed. He never had any trouble talking to Raneen in a Humvee, but suddenly he couldn't think of anything to say.

"Why do you do it, if it is such a dangerous job?" he finally managed.

Raneen's hair had loosened from its bun after a long day, strands curling around her face, and Moge knew suddenly that she had always been a very attractive woman, which explained why she wore no makeup, why she wore a uniform too big and her hair so tightly braided, to try to hide that fact.

She leaned back in her chair. "It pays well," she said softly, and Moge nodded, disappointed. That was the nonpolitical answer all the terps gave but it didn't explain away that interpreters made up more than forty percent of the civilian deaths reported by private contractors and yet they continued to sign up.

Then, as if also embarrassed by her glibness, "I used to work as a secretary in the Economics Department of Baghdad University. It is where I met my husband, but I was fired in 1998 when every woman in Iraq was fired from their government jobs." She sipped at her cup of tea. "It was Saddam Hussein continuing to tighten his already tightened fist, as if trying to get olive oil from an olive pit. Women helped put the Baathists in power, they promised us many things and for a little while it was so. Then Saddam Hussein wanted the approval of the imams, and women could no longer travel without being accompanied by a man, the schools became only single sex, and women began to hide in our homes once again." She touched her hair, tugging at a freed strand. "Now I make more money than my husband ever did. I speak with the Americans and they must respect me because I tell them what the people say and I hope Iraq will soon become safe. Is that not a good reason?"

"Hell yeah," Moge replied. "You ask American soldiers why they're here and they usually say they're saving up for a new Ford truck."

Raneen laughed. They sat like that until the lights flashed off and on in the chow hall the way bars in the U.S. did for last call, with Moge telling her about his life outside of the army, about skyscrapers in New York that left their streets in perpetual shade, about taking his dad's boat out on the Hudson River, about the year he spent studying in England during college. And Raneen told him about her trip to Massachusetts with her diplomat family when she was eleven years old, how she bought a pair of Jordache jeans and a box of scented Magic Markers, how she still remembered the smell of each bright color.

Moge actually got a day off, his first in weeks, and he went to one of the new coffee shops springing up in the relative safety of the Green Zone. He should have been waiting in line for the phone, trying to call Marissa, but instead he took his time reading a London financial newspaper, glancing up over the pages, hoping to see Raneen, to accidentally "bump" into her. He knew she had gone home for the week; the terps worked five weeks on and then had one off, but she had mentioned this place, how it sold the best Turkish coffee and how she would buy a few pounds every month for her family. Then he started to imagine asking her to meet him. Why not? They were friends. It would be good for both of them to socialize outside of the base, away from camouflage and guns, to flip through a newspaper and eat stuffed grape-leaf *dolmas* and not think about war. Yes, he would ask her to meet him and she would smile, showing her crooked front teeth. He thought about it when he fell asleep that night but when she returned to work and he was sitting next to her in the Humvee, he couldn't get the words out of his dry mouth. He told himself that next month he would ask her for sure. He imagined that they would sit close together at the coffee shop, his knee hitting hers under the table, how she would wear a white blouse and he would glimpse her collarbone and her long skirt would reveal her ankles. Maybe she would wear her hair down and it would fall in front of her brown eyes. He never took the fantasy further than that, never held her hand or kissed her throat or unbuttoned her blouse, just sat with her in the shade of a big umbrella, sipping strong coffee, talking.

But the next month he was still shy. And, after her week off, when she didn't return to Liberty, he didn't worry at first. The terps sometimes returned a few days late; there were trips to their extended families and undependable transportation, power outages or funerals or highways that were suddenly closed down. An eighteen-year-old Kurd with halting English rode out with Moge's squad most days.

But after two weeks, each morning hiding his disappointment when the young Kurd showed up at formation, Moge started asking around. "Perhaps her daughter is sick," the other interpreters would say, but Moge felt chilled by their eyes, how they glanced away from his in a way they had never done before. During his patrols, Moge peered down the streets, looking for her tightly woven bun, and he went to the coffeehouse in the Green Zone as often as possible, ordering the Turkish coffee she liked so much, sipping slowly in hopes that she would appear. Once he even went to her quarters. There were two bunk beds but only the bottom of one was made up in white sheets neatly tucked under the mattress. There was a small desk with a stack of books, most in Arabic but also an English dictionary and, oddly, a worn biography of Oprah

Winfrey. There was a cardboard frame that held a photo of a small, serious girl, seven or eight years old, her hair in two dark braids down her shoulders, wearing a starched blouse, standing in front of a brightly tiled doorway. There was nothing else.

Then Khaled returned, fatter since his marriage, bringing a large bag of shelled pistachios and sharing them with Moge and his men as they drove out to check on the shops in Kindi.

"Ah, yes, my wife's family now beg me to be an interpreter." Khaled undid the top buttons on his camouflage. "They say to me, 'Khaled, you were once so rich, now you are like a goat herder,' and I say, 'A rich man must do a dangerous job.' My wife, she cries when I leave for work but she more happy than sad when I return with much money!"

The soldiers laughed.

"Khaled, who is hotter, Angelina Jolie or Nicole Kidman?" Dupont called from the back of the truck.

"Jolie has skin the color of the desert at sunset, and Nicole is like a drowned thing that bruises easily. That is no question, all men with hot blood must agree, yes?"

The guys hooted in approval.

When there was a lull in their talk, Moge leaned into Khaled. "We had a woman interpreter while you were away, Raneen Mahmood. But last month she went home for a few days and never came back. Did they transfer her to another FOB?"

Khaled wiped at the corners of his mouth. "Even a widow, a mother, is not safe."

The muscles of Moge's face tightened. "I don't understand."

Khaled hesitated, Khaled, who never was at a loss for words. The soldiers glanced at each other, listening.

"She is missing," Khaled finally said, carefully wrapping up his bag of nuts so he would not have to look at Moge. "There has been no ransom. Her family no longer has hope she will return." He coughed into his hand. "This is the risk we face. But we must remember it is God's will. *Inshallah.*"

Moge turned away and caught Dupont staring at him, his mouth open, a thin line of tobacco spittle shining on his dark chin. Dupont dumbly moved his mouth as if trying to get enough saliva together to speak or spit but couldn't, then swallowed, lip of chew and all. Moge felt a wave of nausea move through him as if that wad of black was in his own stomach, secreting and rotting. He fastened his eyes on the smudged window of the Humvee. *This is the risk we face.* No one spoke as they rode back to the base.

• • •

Lieutenant Colonel McCormick was making the rounds in the mess hall, eating lunch with a table of privates, asking them for the good word. There had been a big push to stop the soldiers from writing graffiti on the walls of the latrine, and once a week a private was tasked with painting over the new scrawls. Then that private would hold court at the mess and announce to his buddies the clever witticisms he had eradicated.

"Sir, so some guy writes: *Soldiers are like mushrooms, kept in the dark and fed shit.*" The private, as disgusted as he might have been by the morning's work, was now beaming with pride as the colonel put his fist to his mouth and tried not to laugh.

"And below that, sir, someone wrote in big, angry capital letters: *No one tries to blow up a fucking mushroom! I just wanted money for college!*"

The table erupted, laughing more for the lieutenant colonel than for the scribbles.

"Hey, sir?" Moge asked from the end of the table.

"Yes, Sergeant?" Colonel McCormick patted the private on the back and leaned back in his chair.

"Sir, there is an issue I'd like to talk to you about. I brought it up to my company commander but haven't heard anything back."

"Go ahead."

"One of our terps has been kidnapped and we haven't done jack about it." Moge could see his first sergeant stand up from an adjacent table and walk over. Quickly.

The colonel took a sip of his Diet Coke and glanced at Moge's name tag. "Where and when did this happen?"

"From what I could find out, about a month ago, in Salman Pak."

"Hell, Sergeant Mogeson, a month ago? Salman Pak isn't even in our brigade's Area of Operation. Are the Iraqi police or Iraqi Army investigating?"

"Sir, they say they are."

"Is the family cooperating?" The colonel dusted nonexistent crumbs from his uniform.

"I doubt the family will cooperate, sir, since it was the terp's cooperation with American forces that got her kidnapped to begin with."

The colonel pushed his tray away and stood. He glanced at the first sergeant and then back at Moge. "Sergeant, I sympathize. But we found eleven dead bodies on the Ghazaliya Bridge yesterday, and had three separate reports of kidnappings in the last twenty-four hours." He started to collect his trash and when the first sergeant tried to take it, he waved him away. The colonel strode over to the garbage can and jammed his empty cup and crumpled napkins inside.

"But, sir—" Moge ignored the first sergeant's glare.

The colonel straightened, hesitating just long enough to ensure that all of the soldiers were listening. "Look. I don't like dick-dancing around the kidnapping of an interpreter either. Get as much info as you can and I'll pass it on to the Seventh Iraqi Army Brigade commander and ask him to personally get involved. That's the best I can do. But don't hold your breath."

The next day there was a bombing at the market-place in Dora. Moge's squad was patrolling with an Iraqi platoon when the blast went off so close that all of the soldiers' ears were ringing and the sounds of sirens and screams were muted like one of Dupont's gangland video games turned down low.

Their medic was wrapping a tourniquet around the stump of a teenage boy's leg when Moge got the call to get out of the marketplace and report to the FOB immediately.

"Sir, we have to get these people medevaced," he shouted into the radio, barely able to hear whoever was yelling back at him, bits and pieces making it through the echo in his ears.

"Listen, Moge . . . we just got intel . . . secondary IED about to go off . . . trying to lure American and Iraqi troops, ambulances and aid . . ."

"Sir, we can be out of here in ten minutes—"

There was a burst of static, then a new voice came over the radio. "This is Warlord Six." Moge felt the sweat under his armpits go cold. Warlord Six was the call sign of the brigade commander and his voice cut through the chaos loud and clear. "Sergeant, get the hell out of there *now*."

Moge grabbed Doc Riley, his hands covered in blood, got the rest of his men into the Humvee, pulled out with screeching tires while women tried to stand in their path, waving at the black smoke behind them. They drove away in silence, all of them waiting for a second blast that did not come. Doc Riley was rubbing a bloody hand against his forehead, Dupont was tight-lipped in the back of the truck, and Khaled leaned over, his helmeted head in his hands.

"There was nothing we could do," Moge said a few minutes later when there was still no second blast. "If we had stayed, they would have detonated another bomb, more people would have been hurt and killed." He was finding it difficult to breathe and he looked out at gutters choked with raw sewage, flies sticking to the eyes of dead goats suspended in the glassless windows of butcher shops, roads blocked off with cement dividers. There was Arabic graffiti everywhere. Just ahead he saw a crude red, white, and blue American flag with a black X painted through it. He thought of Raneen in her small white room at Liberty, packing up her few belongings before heading home to see her family, her fingers lingering over the photo of her daughter, smiling her crooked smile.

"There was nothing we could do," Moge repeated loudly, as if someone had challenged him, and the guys glanced at each other, still dazed. Moge blinked, the view out the window suddenly too much. He could taste bile in the back of his throat and his ears wouldn't stop ringing, a high, insistent cry that would stay with him for days.

"Marissa? Marissa, I'm sorry to call so late."

He could hear her struggling with the covers of her bed, the click of her lamp, the squeak of bedsprings as she sat up against her wooden headboard. He thought how tightly her hand would be clutching the phone, how she liked telling people that she had been in love with him since the third grade, how once she said she worried about him more than anything else in her entire life.

"What's going on?" she asked breathlessly.

Moge could see her bedroom, the few drawings from her students pinned to a corkboard over her bureau, a framed picture of the two of them drinking margaritas in the Hamptons two summers ago, a stack of gossip magazines by the side of her bed, the whole room smelling of the soapy lilac candles she burned each night.

"I just turned in my final paperwork," he said. "I'll be out of the army a month after I get back. I need you to know that I'm sorry. . . . Can you hear me?"

There was a patch of static as a helicopter lifted from the Camp Liberty airstrip. Moge could see the legs of soldiers dangling as it rose dark and insect-like against the sun-white sky. It seemed impossible that the phone lines could connect this dirty little piece of Baghdad to Marissa's split-level in Long Island, sand swirling around him while she rested in her down-comfortered bed, unchanged and whole.

"David? Are you there? David?" she called into the phone.

"Yeah," he replied. "It's me." He felt everything coming apart, felt himself sweating and shivering at the same time, and he had to sit down in the dust, stretching the phone cord as far as it would go. "It's David." He closed his eyes. "I'm coming home."

He didn't care that there were soldiers watching him, listening, glancing at each other with their foreheads creased, that he was letting them all down. He was getting out, he was going home, and suddenly, finally, that was all that mattered.

REMISSION

Ellen Roddy tried not to stare at the bald-headed, denim-coated baby of indeterminate sex that cried in the chair next to her. The mother faced the baby in the direction of the waiting room's television set but did not attempt any means of comfort, just occasionally broke off a bit of chocolate and shoved it into the toothless mouth. Ellen held her back very straight and resisted figuring out the rank of the woman's husband by her clothes or level of parenting skills. She would not play that game today. Today she was waiting to hear Dr. Pierce's results—the word *results* sounding so innocuous, like the scores from a sporting event rather than the evaluation of Ellen's mortality—and assessing a stranger's rank according to social ineptitude felt like bad luck.

She leaned away from the chocolate-mouthed baby and shivered; the hospital's thermostat was set for the cool comfort of men in layers of camouflage rather than the belly-revealing T-shirted wives and runny-nosed children in the crowded room. She had sped across Fort Hood, racing to arrive in time for her appointment, knowing that if she was fifteen minutes late it would be automatically canceled, and a cancellation meant some mystery major would call her husband and rat her out. That was how the army worked its system of checks and balances; there was an ever-present chain of command, a shadowy specter that haunted the soldier as well as his or her civilian spouse, ready to swoop down with a raised voice and pointed finger at the least infraction.

Then Ellen's cell phone, from the depths of her purse, began to shriek the theme song for *Sesame Street*. Four sets of eyes glared at her from the receptionist desk where a large sign proclaimed TURN OFF CELL PHONES (even the requests in an army hospital were orders, no wasted *please*s here). Ellen searched through balled-up tissues and empty raisin boxes until she found the thin metal phone, glanced at the number, didn't recognize it, then clicked the ringer volume all the way down and stared at her feet, refusing to apologize to the waiting room even with her eyes. When her phone chimed, letting her know that a message was waiting for her, she got up and exited the sliding doors. People who lived in states other than Texas were always telling Ellen, "At least you have a dry heat," which Ellen found insulting. Dry or wet, it didn't matter when the doors opened up to weather that felt like a blowtorch melting off her newly regrown eyebrows.

She dialed her voice mail, pressing the phone to her ear, looking in the window next to the NO WEAPONS ALLOWED placard to make sure Dr. Pierce's nurse wasn't calling her name. There were soldiers mixed among the women and children, some thin with acne scars but most displaying a healthy, broad-chested beauty even in the way they slouched in their chairs. Those waiting with wives were usually better-looking than their spouses, which was the curse of an army base where women were scarce and the enticement to get laid all too often led to the altar. Ellen glimpsed her own image in the glass of the sliding door, her knee-length beige skirt and casually draped blouse. She was thinner now than she had ever been: the bright side to cancer.

There was a message from her daughter's high school secretary, primly informing Ellen that fourteen-year-old Delia was not in attendance and that the principal would like Ellen and her husband, John, to come in and have a chat next week. Their third "chat" in two months.

Ellen snapped the cell phone closed. Last month, during social studies, Delia had been found in the handicapped stall of the girls' room paging through a *Cosmopolitan*. Last week, during biology, she was sitting at the edge of the playground eating a bag of sunflower seeds, spitting the shells on the asphalt. And now this —did kids still call it "playing hooky"?

She took a step forward and just as the automatic doors whooshed her with the morgue-icy air, Ellen's phone rang again. Another unfamiliar local number. She felt a flicker of unease, stepped aside, and answered her phone.

"Hello?"

"Mrs. Roddy, this is Miss Lane from Meadows Elementary School. We need a letter from your son's doctor."

"I'm sorry? Are you calling about Landon Roddy?" Ellen saw Dr. Pierce's nurse enter the waiting room with a clipboard in her hand. She could read the nurse's lips as she enunciated, *Ellen Roddy, Ellen Roddy?* Ellen tapped her knuckles against the glass.

The secretary breathed deeply into the phone as if she had been dealing with inept parents all morning. "Yes. When Landon wasn't at kindergarten attendance and we didn't have the requisite note from you, we called the bus driver. He said your daughter came out of your house, holding Landon's hand, said that he wasn't feeling well, then the two of them walked away. Mrs. Roddy, you know the rules, and your daughter giving a verbal excuse is not acceptable. We need something official in writing."

Ellen's hand slipped off the window and skidded into the rough brick wall of the hospital. "I have no idea what you're talking about. Landon should be at school."

He wasn't. First her fourteen-year-old daughter, now her five-year-old son. Gone.

A young and very thin military policeman, Sergeant Jaboski, met Ellen at her house in Patton Park. His lashes, eyebrows, and hair were so white-blond that the combination of elbows, shoulder bones, and spiky "high and tight" hair-cut made him look like a piece of hot glass. He stood in the center of the living room while Ellen paced around him, recounting how her daughter, Delia, had glared her way through breakfast, storming about the kitchen because Ellen had sliced and sugared strawberries for Landon and not for her. Ellen glanced up at the sergeant, looking for a nod of empathy, a shake of his tenuous head that said, *Yes, I understand what you are going through and I am sure you are a good mother,* but he was too busy scratching ink-smeared notes into his little book.

Ellen continued. She always watched the kids in the morning; of course she had watched them, hadn't she?

"Ma'am?"

But of course she had not, or none of this would be happening. Instead of watching Delia put Landon on his minibus, Ellen had been applying lipstick, twisting her feet into leather flats, buttoning her blouse. Instead of checking on her son and daughter, she had glanced at her watch, hoping she would be on time for Dr. Pierce.

"Ma'am, just to make sure I have this down correctly: you last saw your children when they walked out your front door? You didn't see them get into a stranger's car or anything like that?" Sergeant Jaboski seemed uncomfortable, as if he knew that asking these questions would lodge unpleasant scenarios in Ellen's distraught mind.

"No," she whispered, deciding that it was time to sit down. "I didn't see anything."

The sergeant finally managed to get his spindly limbs out Ellen's front door, refusing her iced tea, coffee, homemade snickerdoodle cookies, and everything else she had tried to make him stay. The authority of his uniform calmed her, but he backed out of the house, smiling and wild-eyed, as if desperate to be inside the safety of his jeep, away from Ellen's near-hysteria.

She watched him drive off, a bit faster than the twenty-five-mile-an-hour residential speed limit, and couldn't help peering out at the guard shack of the East Gate, only a few blocks away, that led to seedy Rancier Street and the huge world outside of Fort Hood's confines. Sergeant Jaboski had told her not to worry, that he would put out the descriptions of the kids on the radio, have the entire MP force do drive-bys across the base, searching all the usual places that teenagers

92

liked to go to (the Captain D's food court on TJ Milnes Boulevard, the arcade at the Warrior Way PX, the matinees and Slurpee machine at Howze Theater). He reminded her that Delia gave the bus driver an excuse for Landon's absence and therefore deliberately took her brother, which meant a stranger had not.

Ellen glanced up at the clock and did the math. It was 10:30—her children had been AWOL now for almost two and a half hours.

The Roddy family problems started about a year ago. Ellen's husband was getting ready to deploy to Iraq when his chain of command found out about Ellen's diagnosis, treatment, and upcoming surgery. It used to be "if the army wanted you to have a family, they'd issue you one," but there had been a perceptible shift as the years of war continued, and in an attempt at familial appeasement, John was appointed the rear detachment commander, a position that allowed him to stay behind. He became the man who handled everything on the home front, from shipping supplies from the States to the forward operating base outside of Baghdad, to approving army emergency loans to families.

So while all of their friends were getting ready to send their fathers and husbands off to war, the Roddys were going to Darnall Hospital. They started to peel away from the army community, a slight unmooring, their foundation coming loose. There was something unseemly about John being home when all the other husbands were not. Not that anyone was overtly jealous of the Roddys, for crying out loud, Ellen had *cancer*. And yet John being home made her different from everyone else in a way that even the cancer did not.

John slept beside Ellen except when a body returned draped in a flag and he traveled to the military funeral. He was there every single night, which might seem normal for civilians but to the military families Ellen knew, it was extraordinary. When neighbors needed a man, they knocked on Ellen Roddy's door and bashfully asked to borrow John yet again—there was a tire that needed changing or a mouse that needed killing or a baseball stuck in the gutter on a roof. Random children who were neither Landon's nor Delia's age showed up on the edge of the lawn on the weekends, hoping that John might emerge with a football or Frisbee. John was a man, that was it, a man inhabiting a military base that was suddenly devoid of its most prominent commodity.

The unit coffee nights and FRG meetings were hell for Ellen; she would sit awkwardly, staring into her lap, while all the women around her commiserated with each other's loneliness, discussed what they ought to send in care packages, or shared the contents of recent letters and e-mails ("Did you hear that they still don't have flush toilets? They're pooping in bags of kitty litter" or "My husband said for us to send flea collars to stop the sand fleas from getting into their cots at night. But tell them not to put the collars around their ankles; if the stuff gets into their skin it'll cause nerve damage"). Someone eventually tried to cheerily change the subject, to ask Ellen how she was feeling, or if John had imparted any secret knowledge that she could share with the group, but anything Ellen said made her more guilty—she was feeling great, actually, look how nice and thick her hair had grown back! or that John was hardly ever home, but how could she complain about that when he was only three minutes away on Battalion Avenue instead of on the other side of the world?

So Ellen stopped going to the events for the spouses. And when Delia started dropping out of things, like soccer, the Art Club, and band, Ellen let her alone. Ellen understood. She imagined Delia was going through the same thing, the sideways glances of the kids at school, the whispers about her father. Delia's dad, in this world of camouflage and guns and absent but heroic fathers, despite his Ranger tab, Combat Infantry patch, and Bronze Star, was not man enough to go to war, instead doing paperwork in a cushy stateside office while other dads were putting their lives on the line.

• • •

Ellen tried John's cell phone again. This time he picked up.

"It's me," she said. "Didn't you get any of my messages?"

John hesitated, as if he was listening to someone else speak to him in his office. "There's been an attack," he finally said. "One dead. Two in the Green Zone ER, one in critical on his way to Germany. It's already hit the news. My phone's been ringing off the hook—wives, parents, reporters—everyone wants to know what's going on."

"Did they release the names?"

"No. We won't be able to contact the families until tonight or tomorrow morning. What's happening at home?"

"Delia took Landon," she said, holding her breath. "They're not in school."

"Thank God." John sighed into the phone. "I thought the doctor had bad news."

Ellen swallowed. She had forgotten all about her appointment. "I never saw Dr. Pierce. Didn't you hear me? Our kids are missing."

"Calm down," he said gently, switching to the voice he used when speaking to the wives who called after hearing about a bombing. "It's just Delia's latest stunt to get attention."

Ellen pressed her fingers into her eyes, the light bursts there oddly soothing.

"She loves Landon. They'll be home soon," John continued. Then his voice stretched as if he had placed the receiver against his shoulder and started to bark out orders to soldiers in the room.

"John?" Ellen's voice took on the same whispered shout she used when they fought just out of earshot of the kids. "The MPs came to the house and are driving around looking for our children. I am going to call the local police, too—"

"Ellen, don't call the cops." He sounded so tired, and suddenly Ellen couldn't remember a time when his placating voice wasn't edged with weariness. "Trust me, the kids are okay."

She could hear his office phone ringing, someone else needing him, something else urgent and dire that he had to deal with.

"I have to go," John said. Before Ellen could reply, he hung up.

Ellen tried not to be angry at John for worrying about soldiers, the children of strangers, more than his own as she drove laps around the streets of Fort Hood: Tank Destroyer, Hell-on-Wheels, Old Ironsides, Audie Murphy Drive. She drove for so long that she was overcome with nausea. She had never had motion sickness or been seasick before being struck with cancer, as if the abnormal and conflagrant cells and their subsequent removal had disturbed her center of gravity, pitching all of her fixed references askew so that even the horizon no longer seemed straight. Then again, when her body began to fail her, when her own breasts seemed to be conspiring to kill her, how could anything else in the world ever seem right?

She parked near the helicopter display outside the First Cavalry Museum, Landon's favorite place, and peered around retired Chinooks and Apaches, praying to see him scaling the monstrous bug-eyed creatures with their admonishing signs of DO NOT TOUCH.

She kept looking for a long blond ponytail and then having to remind herself that Delia was no longer blond. She had come home last month with her long blond hair shorn and dyed black. It still shocked Ellen every time she looked at Delia; it still made her think, *That is not my daughter.* The blond child had never wanted to miss school, even when she was seven and dappled with chicken pox. Now Ellen was searching for someone else, someone sullen and unpredictable. A makeshift roadside explosive device just waiting to go off.

Like that tantrum two weeks before. Ellen was getting dinner ready when Delia came in with a pair of jeans over her arm.

"I told you I wanted to wear these tomorrow," Delia said, knocking into the table and spilling

Landon's milk. "You said you'd wash them."

Ellen took a deep breath, pushing a napkin across the pale white spill. "I'm not going to run the washing machine for one pair of jeans. I told you they'd be clean by the weekend."

Delia stared, mustering a fathomless anger. "If Landon wanted them washed you would have."

So Ellen laughed; it was preposterous that her *five-year-old*, that *anyone* with a closet full of clothing, would demand a particular pair of jeans.

Delia reached across the table, picked up Ellen's mug of green tea, and threw it against the wall, the pottery shattering like a gunshot.

"I wish you had died!" she screamed, her blackened eyes livid with tears. And Ellen, feeling hot tea seep into the back of her blouse, stood there with her mouth open, speechless and scalded.

That night she brought Delia into the laundry room and showed her how to use the washing machine and dryer. Delia stood with her arms tight across her chest, her eyes on the ceiling, ignoring the instructions.

"I'm only fourteen," Delia said. "None of my friends wash their own clothes."

"Well," Ellen returned, flashing her best fake smile, "if I do happen to die, and lucky for you there's still a chance I might, you'll need to know how to do a lot of things, including the laundry."

Delia glanced at her for a moment, her blond eyebrows drawn together, suddenly looking like the child Ellen once knew. Then she shook her head and rolled her eyes. "Whatever."

Ellen continued with her instruction in a singsong voice, but felt slightly dizzy. She had expected Delia to apologize for her outburst. But her daughter, so unrepentant, so coiled against her, was terrifying.

After her search turned up nothing, Ellen went home. She raced up the steps, telling herself that her children had returned and were right now sitting peaceably at the kitchen table, eating the strawberries left over from breakfast. But before she even opened the door she could sense the silence of a childless home, the kind of quiet that she usually longed for, greeting her like a slip into the bathtub, head ducking under the water, warm nothing filling the ears.

The answering machine light was blinking and Ellen tripped over a forgotten box of Texas grapefruit as she struggled to push play.

"Hello, Ellen, this is Dr. Pierce. You had an appointment this morning. We know you signed in at the front desk but you seem to have vanished. I've rearranged my schedule to squeeze you in tomorrow morning at ten—it is important that I give you your results as soon as possible."

Ellen stood with her finger an inch from the red button, fear clouding the corners of the room. What did that mean—it was important that she get the results as soon as possible? That she was clean and he wanted to tell her the good news so she could stop worrying? Or that he had found trace cancer and they needed to aggressively treat it immediately?

When Ellen had first been diagnosed, she had looked up the word *remission* in the dictionary, too proud to ask the doctor for the exact definition of her only hope. *Forgiveness,* she had read, *a decrease in the magnitude of a force,* but not the eradication, just the respite, a second chance. Three months ago Dr. Pierce told her that her body had so far proved resilient, the cancer was in remission (the doctors never said "gone," they never said "cured"), still slumbering deep in her cells, and the longer it stayed asleep the better, and this was the best and only victory for a cancer patient. But she needed to be tested every three months for the first year, and every three months her cancer could once again rise up, alert and terribly awake.

When the high school let out at 3:15, Ellen drove over to the McNair Village Apartments, slanted and gray, with unshaded outdoor parking that baked the paint off the cars lined out front. Crissy Hachett lived there, the daughter of a fellow captain in John's battalion and, lately, one of Delia's closest friends. Every time Ellen saw Crissy she wondered if the girl really had an abnormally small head or if the size was accentuated by the mass of tight cornrows that crossed her pink scalp.

Crissy did not seem surprised to see Ellen at her door, her lip-glossed mouth open as if she tried to cultivate the air of a subpar IQ.

"Hello, Crissy," Ellen said, trying to smile.

"I already told that MP I don't know where Delia is," the girl said, but something in her close-set eyes told Ellen that she did.

"Crissy, dear." Ellen paused around the word *dear* as if it were a threat. She leaned closer and could smell patchouli, which made her frayed temper flash irrationally. When Ellen was in college, the only kids who liked patchouli were the potheads. "Please tell me where my children are or I will immediately inform Sergeant Jaboski that you are withholding information. You wouldn't like the MPs to come to your home and question you again, would you?"

"Mrs. Roddy, if Crissy knew, she'd tell," a quiet voice chimed. Ellen looked beyond the girl and saw the shadow of Mrs. Hachett. She was wearing a T-shirt with a fire-breathing horse that must belong to her husband. It hung past her hips and had a tear at its seam. Ellen stood up as straight as possible. The entire Hachett family was completely at odds with her idea of how an officer's family should behave, with their wrinkled clothes and dented Honda hatchback, never trying to set an example or present their best face to the world. She remembered the Hachetts showing up at a soccer game a few months ago, right before Delia quit the team. They had arrived late, of course, Mrs. Hachett looking harried and windblown in a pair of unflattering shorts and another one of her husband's XL T-shirts. Her chubby ten-year-old son trudged next to her, scabby-kneed with a sore that looked suspiciously like ringworm on his left cheek. Ellen had been cheering on the sidelines and immediately stopped to stare. She was embarrassed. The mangy Hachetts made all the other captain families look bad. Then she saw Crissy, her uniform still grass-stained from a previous practice, saunter over to her mother and throw her arms around her big-breasted girth. Ellen had come early to the game with snacks for the whole team, she and Landon decked out in matching sage Ralph Lauren polos, and she couldn't remember the last time Delia had smiled at her, let alone relinquished herself to a hug.

"It's Ellen Roddy, isn't it?" The woman pushed open the screen and looked Ellen up and down. Ellen tried to remember her name. Martha? "How's your husband doing?"

"Fine," Ellen replied carefully. "And yours?"

"Oh, you know, sick of the desert and missing home." The woman grinned. "No sign of those kids of yours yet, huh?"

Ellen shook her head and tried to stay composed. She wondered what was behind Mrs. Hachett's words—that Ellen had a husband home and still couldn't keep track of her children? She wanted to say something scathing, wanted to fill Mrs. Hachett's smug face with terror, wanted to blurt out that there had been an attack today in Iraq, did the cozy Hachetts know about it? When was the last time they had heard from their soldier? Ellen wanted to wield something over them, anything to wipe that smirk off the lying, pinheaded daughter, who was looking down at her fake-Birkenstocked feet.

"Please call me if you think of anything," Ellen said, imagining how good it would feel to slowly tug those braids until a screaming Crissy released an address, a name. And then she would have liked to kick over Mrs. Hachett's planter of half-dead geraniums. "Here is my phone number."

Mrs. Hachett reached out to take the piece of paper and this time her smile seemed more genuine. "I sure hope they get home soon."

For a moment Ellen thought Mrs. Hachett was referring to her husband and the other soldiers in Iraq, implying that, if he wanted to, John could somehow bring them back tomorrow. Then she realized the woman was talking about Delia and Landon.

"Thank you," Ellen said, hesitating. She looked into Mrs. Hachett's brown eyes and saw relief staring back, relief that this was happening to the Roddys and that the life of the Hachett family, for at least this one day, was still unbroken.

It was almost five when Ellen pulled into her driveway. She had gone to all of the guard gates and asked if anyone had seen a teenage girl and a little boy walk by. She had gone to the five swimming pools, the six schools, and every playground at the housing developments and youth centers. She checked her phone: neither the kindly military police sergeant nor her husband had called her back with an update.

She sat in her car, staring down at the manicured lawns of Patton Park. Three years before, new to Fort Hood, they had lucked out when the housing lottery gave her this home on Marshall Street, in the company and field-grade officer housing, although John was just a junior captain at the time. When they had first moved in Ellen had clapped her hands like a child at Christmas, amazed at the wood fences and picture windows and new hardwood floors, feeling like she and John had triumphed over everyone else whose lottery number had sent them to the smaller, older, shabbier places on post. But now she looked at the thorny rosebushes and weepy pansies lining the street and wondered what was happening within the other immaculate walls, at the dinner tables of other families. Were those children holding hands and saying grace or stonily refusing to eat the meals their mothers had prepared? Pretty Patton Park to tired McNair Village, what were all of those children doing without their dads at the head of their tables, and were the mothers, like Ellen, just barely holding on?

When she finally exited her car, she entered her home slowly, her arms around her chest, no longer hopeful that her children would miraculously be sitting in the kitchen. Inside, Ellen slowly walked into Delia's room. She had looked through it briefly that morning with Sergeant Jaboski. He had wanted to know if Delia had packed a bag or taken her allowance savings. Ellen found twenty dollars in a glass jar under the bed but wasn't sure if that was the extent of her daughter's money. Now Ellen looked around the room again. She just meant to snoop but within minutes she had torn it apart, the drawers upended, the closet gutted so that shoes and jackets spilled out the door, even half of the Harry Potter and teen vampire books pulled down from the shelves, the pages splayed like the feathers of murdered birds.

There was nothing out of the ordinary, no drugs or condoms or cult paraphernalia, just a Marilyn Manson CD that Ellen had expressly forbidden Delia to buy, hidden in a brown paper bag in Delia's sock drawer. Ellen was almost disappointed—she wanted to find something tangible that would explain everything, something that could be fixed, something that could be blamed.

Then the room dipped wildly to the left and Ellen put her hands out, grabbing the edge of Delia's desk to steady herself. Had she eaten anything today? Her heart suddenly seemed to beat so frantically that she thought she could see her blouse moving up and down from the motion. It reminded Ellen of the way the unborn Delia used to kick when trapped in her belly, legs flailing so hard that she could see the outline of miniature feet stretching the skin. Ellen sat down on the floor and took a deep and what she imagined was supposed to be a calming breath. Perhaps this was a case of vertigo, a panic attack, or a heart attack. Something suitably awful that would strike down a woman who couldn't find her own children.

She reached under her shirt, the small silicone bag falling out of the left cup of her bra, and placed her palm over her heart. She tried to count her heartbeats as she breathed. Her hand felt cool against the blank space of her chest, against the rippled, almost slippery scar tissue where she had once had an A cup breast. Ellen couldn't believe how close her hand could be to her heart, how clear and desperate the beat was without the flesh of her breast to mute it, as if she contained some small and wild ocean inside.

Then, almost as if it were an extension of her own internal clamor, she heard keys rattle. She glanced around the mess and stood.

"John?" she called out as she walked shakily toward the front door. John would know what to do; he understood the nature of emergencies, he would take over. And on a deeper level Ellen was glad that his early arrival home meant that he, too, was worried. She knew that against the backdrop of soldiers' lives, of war and insurgent attacks, perhaps the disappearance of their children did not loom large, but this was still a family crisis and she wanted, more than anything, her husband beside her.

But the door swung open and instead Ellen saw Delia holding Landon in her arms, his blond head resting on her shoulder, his mouth yawning and his cheeks red; clearly he had not had his afternoon nap.

"Hey," Delia said, stepping inside and kicking the door closed behind her. She shifted Landon's weight on her narrow hip. "I meant to be home earlier so you wouldn't worry but we took the wrong shuttle bus back—"

Ellen strode across the room and pulled Landon out of her daughter's arms, her wedding ring catching on one of the silver chains hanging from Delia's waist.

Delia's kohl-blackened eyes rolled. "Let me guess, now is when you decide to overreact—"

In a fluid motion, Ellen slapped her daughter's face so hard that she felt the reverberation in her armpit. Delia stumbled backward and Ellen took a deep breath. She wanted to keep slapping so she dropped to her knees and searched Landon instead, her hands moving over his arms and legs to check for injury. Delia disappeared in a flutter of black, running down the short hallway, slamming her bedroom door behind her.

"Are you all right?" Ellen asked. Landon glanced toward Delia's room, pulling out of Ellen's grasp, in some instinctual way aligning his small self with his sister. Ellen tightened her grip.

"It's okay," she whispered, pushing Landon's bangs off his forehead. "Everything is okay now." She took a deep breath; yes, finally, everything was okay. "What did you do today?"

Landon rolled up his right sleeve, revealing a fake tattoo of a heart with the word *Mom* underneath.

Ellen kissed his nose. "That's great."

Landon picked at the ends of the tattoo. "They were out of Spider-Man."

Ellen asked with forced enthusiasm, "Where did Delia take you?" She squinted at him; there were gray marks in the corners of his mouth.

He shrugged, his right hand absently twisting at his fly. "Cory's house. When we got there his dog barked and then peed on the carpet."

"Who is Cory?" Ellen asked.

Landon's eyes widened at the urgency in Ellen's voice. "Can I have ice cream?"

"Landon, who is Cory?"

"Delia's friend." His blond hair had flopped back into his eyes and it made him look crafty. "He put his hand here on Delia." Landon pressed one of his palms against Ellen's chest, on the blank spot, and Ellen leaned away, surprised, realizing that she had not put the silicone bag back into her bra.

"What else did Cory and Delia do?" she asked.

Landon jiggled his fly again and Ellen knew she had only a moment to get him to the toilet.

"Landon, please tell me—"

"They kissed a lot but I made puke noises until they stopped." He threw himself against the wall and started to gag, kicking the white paint until his sneakers left little black smudges.

For a moment Ellen wondered if he was just trying to tell her the most disgusting thing he could think of. "Okay, okay, enough," she said, her voice sharper than she meant it to be, weariness descending on her, the adrenaline of the day gone.

She didn't call Delia out to eat dinner, just microwaved chicken nuggets and canned corn for Landon. Afterward Ellen bathed her son, checking behind his knees and under his armpits for bruises of any kind but finding nothing, nothing but chocolate crumbs, and he told her he ate almost a whole package of Oreos until Delia took them away and made him watch a TV show about squids that he didn't like.

"Cory's house was fun," Landon whispered as Ellen tucked him into bed, running her fingers through his damp hair. She kissed his forehead, leaving her lips pressed near his hairline until he moved away, nestling deep under his covers. Ellen knew that soon he wouldn't let her kiss him goodnight anymore, that there was a time limit on a child's affection, that each year, month, week, day, whittled away at it until he, too, would stretch and grow out of childhood and into something prickly and strange.

Ellen felt her face redden as she crossed the hallway between the bedrooms, passed the school pictures that showed the devolution of Delia from blond braids in the first grade to black-lipped frown in the most recent. Ellen hadn't wanted to buy the photo but John said they had to show Delia that she couldn't shock them, that they would love her nonetheless, and maybe Delia would realize how ridiculous she looked if she had to walk by that picture every day. But the photo angered Ellen every time she saw it, with the dog collar, yes, *dog collar,* on Delia's throat; every time Ellen saw it she felt as if her daughter were laughing at her. Ellen's back straightened and her fists clenched and she knew she was not going to back down this time; there might be yelling but Ellen was the mother, she was resolute, she would ensure this did not happen again. She remembered when she was young and misbehaved, how her own mother would say to her, "I love you but right now I do not *like* you," but right now Ellen felt nothing, nothing at all except rage, and she wondered if it was possible to reach the end of a mother's love.

Delia's room was dim, lit only by a desk lamp with a purple scarf tossed over the bare bulb even though Ellen always told her it was a fire hazard. Ellen hesitated in the doorway and looked at the shipwreck of Delia's room, all of her things ransacked and exposed. Delia was washed up on the shore of her bed, curled into the fetal position, her back to the door.

Ellen leaned over to pick up the strewn black clothing. She remembered dressing a tiny Delia in pink dresses and wide-brimmed hats and how strangers would come over to them in the grocery store and tell Ellen how beautiful her baby was. How proud Ellen had felt at her small daughter holding court and doling out smiles to her admirers.

"What were you thinking?" she asked, tears suddenly distorting her vision. "I called the MPs. I drove around post and talked to your friends—"

The body on the bed shifted, the spine straightening out, the dark head lifting as if from a deep sleep.

Ellen continued, trying to keep her voice low so she didn't wake Landon but she could feel it rising, bouncing off the postered walls and low ceiling, caught in the shadows of the room and gathering under the unmade bed like a rising tide. "You put your brother at risk, you put yourself at risk. Who is this Cory? I can have him arrested for kidnapping. I can have *you* arrested for kidnapping. I didn't know if you and Landon were alive or dead—"

Delia sat up, the purple light ghoulish on her pale cheeks. "You didn't know if Landon was alive, right? You were only worried about him." Her voice sounded tired and thin, much older than it should have.

Ellen took a step closer, her hand to her forehead. "Where were you?"

Delia leaned against the headboard with a sigh. "Comanche One."

The Comanche I and II developments were on

113

the other side of the base, older town houses and duplex-housing areas, with cracked shutters, air conditioner units crooked in the windows, and chain-link fences around the small yards. Ellen had driven around there four times.

Delia continued, "Cory's mom was working. We watched TV and ate cookies; we were like a family. It was good."

Ellen was speechless. Again she wished John was there. He would know what to say, he would be calm and rational, his voice stern as he laid out Delia's punishment, the extra chores, coming home directly after school, no phone privileges, then a talk about sex, the horrors of teen pregnancy and STDs, maybe even make her watch that video about suppurating genitals he forced his single soldiers to sit through before and after a deployment. But Ellen felt tears in her eyes and her throat was so full she didn't know if she could even speak. She sat down on the corner of her daughter's bed and put her hands to her face.

"Why did you do this to me?" she finally managed, her body shuddering. She had not cried like this all year, not even when they first told her she had cancer or that she would lose her breast; no, then she had nodded and told herself that everything would be okay. But now nothing was okay, this child sitting across the bed from her was a mystery, a punishment, incomprehensible. So Ellen sobbed. She felt the bed shift, felt Delia moving her legs, sliding over the bedsheets, coming closer like an animal in the night.

Ellen slid her hands from her eyes and turned on her daughter quickly, as if trying to catch her doing something wrong, but Delia had crept close and was just sitting there breathing, her pupils enormous in her eyes. Then she held her hands toward Ellen, her palms cupped together, and it looked as if they were filled with water.

"This was on my floor," Delia whispered.

Electricity shot through Ellen's spine when she realized that Delia was holding the small silicone bag, her simulated lost breast. Ellen snatched it away, heat rising up her neck, and formed a fist around the jellied warmth.

"Mom, what did the doctor say?"

Ellen blinked. Had she told the kids about the appointment? She didn't mean to, she didn't want them to worry. Then she remembered the fight over the jeans, how she had told Delia that she still might die, how she had let her own fears seep out and into her daughter.

Delia looked down at her now empty hands and then put a thumb to her dark lips. Her fingernails were painted black but the polish was chipped as if she had gnawed away at it. "What were the results?"

"I don't know," Ellen said carefully, taking a

deep breath and staring at her daughter's mutilated fingertips. Could Ellen have been the cause of such worry? Did Delia imagine a motherless life ahead, one in which she would have to care for Landon? "Your school called before I saw the doctor and I immediately started looking for you. I'll find out tomorrow."

Delia lifted her face, the eyeliner rubbed into bruised-looking circles under her blue eyes. "I'm sorry, Mom," she whispered, her voice unsure. "I'm so sorry."

Ellen lifted her arms and Delia flinched as if expecting another blow. Instead Ellen violently pulled her daughter into her chest, clasping her so tightly that Delia's cheek was pressed into the bone of Ellen's ribs, into the place that had once been soft but was now stripped bare, and Ellen's head pressed into her daughter's neck, feeling the pulse where Delia's neck and shoulders connected.

They stayed like that in the darkened, dismantled room, Delia's ear against her mother's heart, trapped and holding tight, both astounded by the pounding of the other's blood, the life in each of them as unknown, as magnificent and as frightening, as the sea.

INSIDE THE BREAK

The buses were blue. There was a long line of them lurking, heaving in that big circus-animal way, giving off exhaust, shuddering, making their presence known, devouring the scant minutes left to the families. When the six hundred uniformed soldiers gathered into a sea of digitized green, Kailani Rodriguez and the other Bravo Company wives drew together. They watched their soldiers stand at attention behind the red banner of unit colors, then march into the waiting buses. The women waved and finally let themselves cry, holding tight to the children who wanted to run after their fathers.

Cristina Diaz nudged Kailani and pointed away from the men, who were turning back for a final thumbs-up before boarding. Kailani followed Cristina's perfect fingernail as it pierced the air to the left, a hot pink arrow centering on the supply company bus.

"What?" Kailani asked. She didn't know any of the supply soldiers; they were "non-combat" forces, all the cooks, mail clerks, mechanics, truck drivers, and forklift operators who would work at the forward operating base, or FOB, in Iraq.

Most of them wouldn't go beyond the wire like her infantry, trigger-pulling, rifleman husband, Manny. Now, thanks to Cristina's distraction, when Kailani looked back at her husband's bus, she could no longer distinguish Manny's head among so many short-haired others.

"Look!" Cristina's voice was tear-free and loud. The other wives glanced at her and then followed the line of her lifted arm. They didn't appreciate being disturbed from their grief either, the tears streaming, rivulets in the thick makeup on their cheeks, mascara pooling under their eyes, noses running. It was fine to look this horrible now that the men were too far away to see their faces, fine to finally grieve, messy and ugly. Crying in public offered a strangely satisfying relief. Most of them had been through this before, the good-bye, the long deployment, the jubilant return, and they cried now as much for themselves and the lonely year ahead as they did for the men heading off to the dangers of war. Even the most stoic women, the three German wives, standing next to each other as always, thought of the diapers they would be single-handedly changing for three hundred and sixty-five days, the dogs to walk and goldfish to flush, the garbage to take out, the anniversaries they would be celebrating without their mates, and they pushed Kleenex against their noses as desperately as the youngest, most sensitive spouses.

Except for Cristina. Cristina stood there in her pink tank top while everyone else had tried to put on something red, white, and blue, or maybe a sunny "I'll be waiting" yellow. Cristina, rigid-backed in her hooker-heels, her perfect head of hair not moving in the wind.

"Look. *Mira!*" she said, and it was as if she lit a match, the flicker of its light illuminating each woman's face as they turned and followed that knife-tipped nail and watched the supply soldiers trickle into their bus. The wives, pausing in their tears, eyes peering, lips biting, wiping at their faces with the back of their hands, glancing at each other, their grief forgotten and filled with a new wariness.

"Twelve?" Rosie Rosado asked, shaking the baby on her hip.

"Fifteen," Cristina said, finally dropping her arm to her side with a chime of sliding bracelets.

All the wet eyes watched that final bus, how it revved its engine to keep up. That supply bus held a threat that had never occurred to any of them when they thought of faraway insurgents and bombs and helicopters crashing.

That supply bus with its fifteen women.

Ten and a half months into the deployment was marked with a long and ominous silence, longer than any other.

Not one wife of Bravo Company, not one wife

of the entire battalion, received a call or e-mail from her soldier for three days. There had been silences in the past that usually meant there had been an attack. They called it a "comms blackout" when the FOB shut down all communications: phone, Internet, e-mail, even confiscating the local Iraqi cell phones that some of the U.S. soldiers were starting to buy and hide under their cots. Finally, on day four, the rear detachment commander, Captain Roddy, initiated the telephone roster that existed in each company's FRG, the wives calling each other in a carefully connected DNA strand, repeating an approved script to separate fact from fiction, hushed voices reassuring the wife at the other end that her husband was okay.

Cristina was tasked with calling Kailani. "Alpha Company got hit," she said calmly. "Sergeant Schaeffer died."

Kailani blinked. This wasn't any script she had heard before, this was Cristina being Cristina and unable to soften shock, unable to resist delivering a punch line without euphemism or explanation. Kailani felt a murky terror and relief —she remembered meeting Sergeant Schaeffer at the battalion farewell barbecue, how he had joked about not being able to swim as he hefted his muscled self onto the rickety dunking booth, letting all of his soldiers take aim over and over again, plummeting him into a tank of contaminated-looking water. Cristina's voice continued, "They got two soldiers at the Baghdad ER with burns, another in Germany in critical condition, but Captain Roddy, he say they all gonna make it." There was a long pause, Kailani still too frightened to speak.

"You still there, Kailani? You hear me? I said it was Alpha; Bravo is fine. Our guys had to secure the blast site, but they okay. They gonna call home any day now."

But Manny didn't call.

By day seven, when there was still no word from Manny, Kailani put her three-year-old daughter down for her nap, her thirteen-month-old son in his pack 'n play, and paced the living room, braiding and unbraiding her long hair as she considered her options. Could Cristina have been wrong? Maybe Manny was one of the soldiers in the Baghdad ER, burns on his legs and arms, too hopped up on meds to remember her phone number? She could telephone Cristina, ask if she had heard anything new, if the comms blackout was officially over, or if Cristina had heard from her man yet. But if Cristina *had* spoken with her husband, then she would know that something was up with Manny. Cristina worked at a salon, gossiping and inhaling nail polish fumes, and Kailani didn't want to be one of her woozy topics.

So Kailani sat down at the computer and,

convinced it was the only thing she could do, broke into Manny's e-mail. It wasn't hard. He had used the same password for as long as she had known him: *MonsterManE*.

She accessed his account and glanced down the page, seeing her past missives *ARE YOU OK?????, Javier took two steps today!!!* and yesterday's *E-MAIL ME ASAP,* all the while feeling something growing behind her lungs, something that wanted to swallow the air inside of her. Most of the e-mails had not been opened yet, but her husband had definitely been online: a message from one of his high school friends, dated just two days before, was no longer in the New Mail section. At that point she ought to have clicked the mouse on the little *x* in the corner of the screen, ought to have leaned back in relief, certain he was fine. But she felt the thing in her chest expand, and she continued skimming over the messages that Manny had read. There was one from his brother, a forward from another buddy from home, something she hoped was junk mail advertising pictures of Britney Spears's crotch, and one from a name she didn't recognize, a michelle.c.rand@us.army.mil, titled *So lonely*. "@us.army.mil" was tacked onto every active-duty soldier's name as an e-mail address. The mouse hovered, the little arrow pointing at *So*. Who was this Michelle Rand and why was she telling Manny she was lonely?

Kailani clicked *Open*:

Manuel,
Are u coming over tues? My roommate is on duty we will have the whole nite. I want ur body so bad.
Let me no asap.
Shell

Kailani pushed her chair away from the desk and stared at the computer screen, at the jeering cursor pointing at *ur body so bad*. She felt a stillness overtake her; she could hear nothing but blood beating in her ears like the surf—no other sound, no breath, no life. She dropped her head on the keyboard and tried to inhale. Then she stood up so fast she felt dizzy, overturning her chair and making Javier squeal with joy at the noise of it hitting the linoleum. Kailani needed to move, to act; if she didn't do something immediately she would never be able to breathe again.

She leaned over and clicked the mouse on *Reply*, a portal opening up between her shaking fingertips and somewhere dark and wrong so far away. She began to type faster than she could think:

Listen bitch, Manny is my husband you stay away from him or else.

I am telling his chain of command I know who you are MICHELLE RAND. You are a whore.

From,
Manny's Wife and the Mother
of his two Children

Kailani clicked *Send* and then immediately flipped the switch on her computer, not bothering to shut down the Internet connection, just pressed hard as if it had somehow become an evil thing and she had to kill it. She looked over at her son hitting two rattles against each other over and over again, grinning up at her, glad to have reclaimed her attention. She smiled back, tears blurring her vision until he was a swirl of noisy underwater color in the middle of the room.

That night, after putting Javier and Ana to sleep, Kailani tried to get into her husband's e-mail again. The password *MonsterManE* was now invalid. So she went to bed in her clothes, not even taking off her sneakers, feeling the underwire of her bra poking her skin.

Her husband was all right. The knowledge no longer offered relief. She shifted under the blankets, her fingers and toes cold, as if her blood had left her extremities in order to fill her heart instead. Manny had been blown up once, during his first deployment, before Kailani had known him. A car loaded with explosives had careened into his checkpoint. He had been lucky, just got scarred by flying shrapnel. Four years ago those scars drew Kailani to him when they met on a beach in Hawaii, those lines in the middle of his handsome face drawing a map down his throat and curving under his right shoulder, an outline of where his Kevlar could not protect him, a path of history and mortality that she longed to follow with her fingers and mouth. She had wanted to make that marked flesh, that foreign land, her own. And now that land belonged to someone else.

Manny called an hour later. Kailani hadn't been sleeping, just lying in bed staring at the ceiling with tears burning down both sides of her face, still curling and uncurling her toes for warmth.

"Did you hack into my e-mail?" he asked as soon as she picked up.

"Hacked? I used your password." Her voice was slow and she felt too tired to talk, let alone muster the anger she needed for the situation.

"Thank God it was you," Manny said, and Kailani blinked, preparing herself for his excuse. There was always an excuse, sweet-talking, honey-tongued Manny. "I thought it was someone from the outside playing with me, you know?" he continued quickly. "I thought I was going to have to report a leak to Operations Security. I thought I was gonna be in big trouble."

"You don't think you're in *big trouble?*" Kailani whispered back, her voice strained, wanting to shout but careful of the kids in the next room. "I've been worried sick about you, that you were hurt in that attack. I just wanted to know if you were okay and then I find out—"

"That's the crazy part." Manny actually laughed. "You're not going to believe how crazy this is."

Kailani said nothing. She looked at her closet. She had taken out a suitcase earlier and opened it up on the floor but hadn't put anything inside it. She also hadn't called her mother or her friends. They would tell her what they always told her: to leave him, to return to Hawaii, to get back to where she and her children belonged.

"Kay, listen to me. This is all a mistake. The lady who sent me that e-mail, she got some boyfriend in the army named Manuel Rodriguez, but he ain't me. She just type in my army address thinking it's him, get it? I e-mailed her back already a few days ago and told her she had the wrong guy. And then you e-mailed her! Man, she write me right away and was real upset and apologetic. Crazy, huh?"

Still Kailani was silent.

"You know how many Mexicans there are in

the army? C'mon, don't be like this. You know there's even another Rodriguez in my company! It's Spanish for Smith." He tried to chuckle. To chuckle, for goodness' sake, as if that were the secret to winning her over. Kailani sat up in the bed and looked again at the suitcase, lying there as if its arms were wide enough to embrace her entire life. She would pack, damn it. She would pack and be home by the weekend, waking up to the ocean every morning, falling asleep to it every night. Then Manny's voice dropped low and Kailani imagined him standing in the front of a long line of impatient soldiers tapping their boots and eyeing their watches, his machismo blushing as he whispered, "Baby, I love you. I would never cheat."

"I'm going to find out," Kailani finally said. "I'm going to call the Family Readiness Group leader and ask if there is a Michelle Rand on your FOB. I'll find out, Manny, you'll see."

He took a deep breath and for a moment there was static, and Kailani thought they had been disconnected. Then his voice came back, distorted at first and then normal again. "—do that. But it's all some twilight zone mistake. I gotta go, the captain's waiting on me, we're about to go on patrol to find the fuckers who lit up Alpha. Tell me you love me before I hang up."

Kailani held the phone against her forehead, inhaled, and put it back to her ear.

Manny's voice was begging. "You love me, you know you do. But you got to say it, baby, or I can't hang up." He waited, breathing loudly into the phone. They never hung up without saying those words, fighting or not. It was their unspoken acknowledgment that at any moment Manny could be blown into thousands of gory pieces. Kailani thought of Sergeant Schaeffer— what had his wife said to him the last time they spoke on the phone?

"Be safe," she whispered. Then she closed her eyes and said in a low, broken monotone, "I love you."

When Manny first left for Iraq, Kailani's family had asked her to move back to Hawaii for the twelve-month deployment, but she knew that while there was not *one* thing that could compare to her love for her husband, *all* of the details of the island of Oahu would conspire against him. The avocado trees in her mother's backyard, the scent of plumeria after a mid-afternoon rain, the black-and-yellow myna birds heckling traffic as they strutted across the street, the sun setting over the sand while sea turtles rested in the shallows. All of the islands would be begging her to stay, and she did not know if she was capable of leaving them again.

So Kailani had held out these eleven land-locked months in central Texas, living in an apartment building on base with her potted hibiscus, the leaves yellowing, the buds small and crinkled, moving it around each afternoon to the three small windows in the living room trying to catch the sun. Her children in a playpen rather than growing up with sand between their toes or sea salt drying in their hair. Her baby, Javier, had never seen the ocean, and Ana wouldn't go into the pools on post without her Little Mermaid floaties bulging around her arms, afraid of the sting of chlorine in her eyes. When Kailani was Ana's age, her mother had already taken her surfing at Nanakuli Beach. Little Kailani would be perched at the front of the board, her long hair touching the water while her mother paddled out and found the perfect wave to ride in, then stood with loose knees while Kailani squealed at the sudden speed.

When she missed Oahu the most, Kailani forced herself to imagine Manny back safe, his arms lifting up his baby boy, his low voice singing Spanish songs to Ana while she sucked her thumb and her lids grew heavy with sleep, his mouth on Kailani's throat in the dark bedroom. He was her island, her ocean, her trade wind breeze. Until michelle.c.rand@us.army.mil.

Kailani drove her children to the Family Readiness Center. A month before she had signed up for a long-awaited video conferencing slot.

The three of them would get to talk to Manny through a television screen for a whole half hour. Kailani had been excited about this "date" with her husband for weeks. Now she considered not showing up, leaving Manny to sit in Iraq in front of a blank screen to demonstrate the uncertainty of their future. But she woke that morning and donned her prettiest dress, a red birds-of-paradise print with spaghetti straps, and buttoned the kids into the matching Hawaiian shirts that her mother had sent especially for the occasion.

"Wow, you guys are beautiful," Manny said, his lips moving slightly out of sync with his words. Ana reached out to try to touch the screen.

"Hey, baby girl," Manny said. "You getting so big. And look at our little man, he almost not even a baby no more."

Kailani fretted over the collar of Javier's shirt, refusing to look at her husband. Her anger felt like a meek case of static cling, more annoying and cloying than the galvanizing rush of electricity and fire she had expected. She rubbed her legs and twitched her hair nervously, anything but make eye contact.

"You look great, Kay," Manny said.

She faced the image in front of her, about to say, "Do I look as good as Michelle Rand?" but the sight of Manny unsettled her, left her with her lips parted, forgetting to breathe. He looked too thin. His hair, which he had always kept as long as regulations allowed, had been completely shaven, the stubble on his scalp a grayish-blue. Even with the screen's poor resolution, his old scars looked livid and new.

Manny waited for her reply, smiling so hard Kailani wondered if his cheeks were aching from the effort.

"You not still thinking about that e-mail?" he asked in a lowered voice, glancing offscreen and rubbing the smile away with his knuckles. "I told you the truth about that: it was a mix-up. Do you want me to change my password back so you can check my account whenever you want? I'll do that. I'm not hiding anything."

"You've had days to erase all the messages," Kailani said. "Of course you have nothing to hide."

"I'll be home in less than a month." Manny leaned forward and his head was suddenly blurry and too big. Ana hid her face in her mother's hair. "Kay, you got to believe me. I love you. I love my babies. We got a good marriage. I'm gonna be home soon and I'll prove it to you. Okay? One month."

Kailani shrugged. "Talk to your daddy." She pinched her daughter, who remained shy, sucking her thumb. "Tell him about the neighbor's puppy." Ana nodded and in an incomprehensible three-year-old babble, told Manny about the Jack Russell terrier next door.

A red light blinked over the screen when their half hour was up.

"I'll be home soon," Manny repeated, and Ana blew kisses at the screen while Javier tried to swallow his curled fist. "You better be waiting for me, Kay. Please."

Kailani tipped her chin in a noncommittal nod and picked up the toys that littered the table in front of her.

It was strongly recommended that all the spouses, from the battalion commander's wife to the newest private's eighteen-year-old bride, attend the Redeployment FRG Meeting. When Kailani walked in, Cristina beckoned with her rhinestone-studded fingernails. Kailani joined her and the other wives of Manny's closest buddies, what he called his Mexican Connection: Diaz, Sanchez, Garcia, Rosado. Their wives were welcoming but their first language was Spanish and they always reverted back to it. Kailani would watch them, how they leaned into each other, their quick whispers and laughter, and it made her yearn to be home, to have such an understanding, to be a part of a whole.

When Captain Roddy stood, women stopped chatting and straightened in their fold-up chairs. He always seemed slightly uncomfortable with the spouses, with the niceties involved with dealing with women, the feelings that could be hurt, the hope of good news in the waiting eyes. He glanced around the room as if he wished he were in Iraq, briefing a roomful of infantry meat-eaters, cursing his head off and spitting tobacco into a battered Coke bottle.

"We've had a dark day," he began. "Please keep the Alpha Company soldiers and their families in your prayers."

Then, looking relieved, he handed the floor over to the chaplain, who began a digressive talk about the Resurrection, which veered into the benefits of families praying together, which somehow led to PowerPoint slides about marriage counseling, and finished with him exhorting everyone in the room to attend at least one counseling session when the soldiers returned. A colonel with a medical branch patch stood beside the chaplain, nodding his head, and then showed some PowerPoint slides of his own about how to spot post-traumatic stress disorder. Finally a pregnant sergeant from Finance, her desert camouflage pant bottoms tucked into white sneakers and her uniform jacket straining over her massive belly, went over everything from balancing checkbooks to telling them not to let their husbands spend all their deployment savings on new trucks.

Cristina elbowed Kailani and shouted loudly enough for the entire auditorium to hear, "New truck my ass. We're spending that deployment cash on me!" The wives laughed maniacally and much too long, as if completely broken by the deluge of bad news and desperate to think about anything else. They started shouting out random desires, "Pedicure!" "Nanny!" "Liposuction!" "Toddler muzzle!" "Boob job!" until Captain Roddy stood up with a look of such disgust that the wives, afraid he was about to tell them about a new attack, immediately shut up and hunched their shoulders protectively.

"I want to thank you once again, on behalf of our soldiers, for your continued love and support," he said. Staring, it seemed, at Cristina, as if he were imagining making her do push-ups until all of her fuchsia nails fell off. "Our soldiers couldn't do their jobs over there if they were weakened with worry about all of us over here."

As the women filed out, their momentary giddiness forgotten, the battalion FRG leader, Bonnie McCormick, stood at the door and thanked everyone for coming, smiling widely as if they had all just gotten free aromatherapy massages rather than descriptions of how emotionally stunted and easily angered their long-lost mates may be. Kailani hesitated at the exit. She could pull Bonnie aside and ask her to find out if there was a Michelle Rand at the men's forward operating base. She knew the army took adultery seriously, especially if two soldiers were involved; there could be demotions, pay loss, transfers to other bases.

Kailani had never asked Bonnie for anything before, though she had often made sweet Hawaiian bread stuffed with pineapple jam for FRG bake sales, bought the requisite raffle tickets, helped wash cars, and everything else the FRG had asked of her. She could ask Bonnie to do this small thing; she didn't even need to mention adultery, just find out if there was a Michelle Rand at the FOB.

But Kailani walked right by Bonnie McCormick without even making eye contact, fleeing the meeting, not even saying good-bye to Cristina, Maria, Fran, and Rosie, who stood in the parking lot chatting in rapid Spanish, hands moving like moths in the dim streetlights.

Kailani would wait. Manny would be back in a couple weeks. She would talk it all out with him in person. Wasn't that the mature thing to do, the married thing to do? She didn't want his superiors, or anyone else, to know their business, and maybe, just maybe, Manny was right.

Maybe it had been a big mistake.

There had only been one time, in all the years they'd been together, that Kailani asked Manny about his scars. They were sitting on a towel at Waiamea Bay, drinking bottles of warm Longboard Lager, watching the sunset and a few surfers out on the water. Kailani could tell they were a bunch of newbies by the way they were paddling frantically and kept missing the waves.

Manny put his arm around her, and she rested her cheek on his shoulder, peering at the line in his throat. "Did a car bomber do that to you?" she asked, so close she could see the little pink pinpricks where the thread had stitched the skin back together again.

"That's what you civilians say." He glanced at her. "The army officially calls them 'suicide vehicle-borne improvised explosive devices.'"

He rubbed at the scar with his palm, almost hitting her with his elbow, but she couldn't help herself. "Did you see it coming?"

Manny shrugged. "This was early in the war. We didn't have all the barriers and shit we have now. We didn't think the sonabitches would blow themselves up." He stood up and shook sand from his shorts. "I was in front of our check-point waving down traffic, and this car sped right by me. I could see the driver. I could have shot him if I had a clue. Shit, I could have reached out and punched him in the face, he was so close."

Manny kept his eyes on the black figures paddling out. He certainly wasn't a local, but he was athletic enough not to make an ass of himself when he was in the water. Like Kailani, he knew that only an expert or an idiot would surf Waiamea at this moment, the tide high and deadly. She stood up next to him. It didn't take long for two of the surfers to get trapped inside the break, the waves roiling full force on top of them, and as they tried to swim forward they kept getting shoved under again by the next wave. It had happened to Kailani often enough, each wave crashing on top of her just when she thought she'd made it out and could take a deep breath. Instead she would get all turned around, not knowing which way was up, and swim down toward the sand, choking, or come up just to get pummeled again. She knew she had to keep her cool, keep trying to paddle until she made it to the other side, surfacing in the undulating waters just beyond the point where the waves were set loose and wild upon the shore.

Manny started pacing, looking as if he was about to wade in and drag the surfers to the beach, when they finally paddled through and emerged on the smoother side, bobbing on their boards, high-fiving and coughing up sea salt.

When Manny and Kailani got to his car, the parking lot dark and quiet except for the slapping noise of a surfer peeling his wet suit from his skin, Manny continued as if their conversation had never been interrupted. "Afterwards there was blood everywhere. You couldn't tell the bits that were American from the bits that were the bomber. Everything was all mixed up."

Manny tried to smile as if he had told her some sort of joke, and, awkwardly, Kailani smiled, too. She reached out and put her hand on the place where his neck and shoulder met, trying to feel the damaged, puckered skin under his T-shirt. He'd been promoted to sergeant and was getting transferred to Fort Hood soon, and she had assumed their relationship would end when he left. But, standing in that parking lot, talking about death, knowing he had been close to it and survived, she wanted to marry this man. She wanted to give up her islands for him and his scars.

The Manny who walked into the auditorium, his uniform stiff with dried sweat, his cheekbones gaunt, hunched beneath his camouflage assault pack, was a different man from the tan and wide-shouldered soldier who had swaggered into his blue bus just twelve months ago. But Kailani spotted him immediately; she knew her husband's walk; she knew the brown eyes that he turned on the cheering crowd, squinting, until he found her holding Javier up in the air, Ana at her side jumping up and down and waving a teddy bear dressed in camouflage. He had to stand at attention in formation with everyone else until the pounding music stopped and then the battalion commander, Colonel McCormick, limped across the room and said a few words about bravery and blood and keeping America free; but Kailani was too busy holding on to her children to listen to his words.

The colonel released the soldiers and the formation broke down into a swarm of uniforms and searching men, women bursting through the ranks to jump into the arms of their husbands, mothers touching their grown sons' smooth faces, vets and fathers walking around shaking hands, children screaming and laughing and veering wildly into the legs of daddies who were strangers.

Kailani waded through the bodies, shushing Javier, who, frightened by the mayhem, cried into her hair. Then Manny was there, smiling so wide that, in his suddenly thin face, it seemed as if he had too many teeth, and Ana pulled Kailani's skirt over her face and Javier started screaming louder. Kailani had meant to stay aloof, had meant to stay out of Manny's arms until she was sure they had never been around anyone else, but instead she collapsed against her husband, pressing her face to his uniformed chest. She knew she was smelling the sand of the desert, but it felt as if she was breathing in the air of a sun-baked beach.

Kailani kept putting off the conversation about michelle.c.rand@us.army.mil. Of course she

139

didn't want to ruin Manny's return, his reunion with his children. The next day, after he had slept for thirteen hours straight, woken up famished, gratefully eaten her fried eggs over Spam and white rice, kissing whatever part of her came near the kitchen table—her hip, her shoulder, her wrist—well, she couldn't bring it up then, either, while he was so happy and the kids were starting to get used to him. Ana had finally whispered, looking between the framed photograph that she had been carrying around for the past few weeks and Manny's ashen face, "Daddy?"

He checked in at work on the third day. He had to attend a week of army counseling, then classes about reestablishing himself in a family and handling the civilian world. Kailani found the pamphlets from the most recent brief and read through them while Javier and Ana napped. They had titles like "Roadmap to Reintegration," "What to Expect When Deployed Soldiers Return," and "Communicating with Your Spouse," and were filled with lots of glossy photos of families reunited.

She scanned the bold print of "Things a Soldier Should Remember":

No cursing.
Your family members are not your men;
    they are not your squadron or platoon;
    they do not have to obey your orders.

Your wife has been handling the finances and disciplining the children during your absence. Do not expect to suddenly walk in and take over. Work with her, and most importantly, tell her you appreciate her and that she has done a good job.

Expect that it will take about six weeks to adjust to each other again. If you are not getting along well at the end of six weeks, counseling might help.

Take time to be charming!

There was a section on the back that made her blush with relief when she read it, glad to know why her wolfish husband had not yet molested her: *Psychologists recommend that you do not engage in intercourse with your wife immediately upon return. Wait a few days until she shows signs of responding to you. BE PATIENT!!!*

Manny came home from work that night with a six-pack of beer, and they drank a few with dinner, making eyes at each other while Ana ate her dinosaur-shaped chicken nuggets and Javier chased his peas around with chubby fingers. Manny helped with Javier's bath, squirting his wife with the rubber ducky, then whistling when she knelt down at the side of the tub.

As soon as the children were in their beds,

Manny turned off all the lights in the apartment and Kailani was touched to see that he had lit candles in the bedroom (*be charming!*). When he kissed her, his lips were shier than they had ever been, and for a moment she was disoriented, as if feeling a stranger's mouth. Then Manny's hands slid down the sides of her waist as if he owned her, and she let him lead her to their bed, let him lay her down, let him back into her life completely.

Kailani was woken by Manny moving next to her. She blinked in the dark, thinking her husband was ready for more. But when she rolled over and looked at him, she saw him flailing, his hands searching through the sheets tangled around him.

"Manny, wake up," she said gently. She wasn't sure if she should touch him, if she should startle him awake, and she backed away, afraid that his elbow, his knee, his fist, would land on her as he wrestled with the blankets.

He opened his eyes. His arms hovered in the air for a moment, then dropped to his sides. "Shit. I thought I was in my tent. I didn't know what was wrapped around my legs." His voice was hoarse. "I was freakin' out 'cause I couldn't find my rifle."

Kailani watched her husband's profile, the thin glitter of sweat on his forehead, his chapped lips. She edged closer. "Do you want me to get you some water, some milk?"

He shook his head. Then he turned toward her, his eyes shining in the red light of the alarm clock. For a moment she thought he didn't recognize her, that he was expecting a different woman to be next to him. Kailani sat up and pulled the sheet against her breasts, helplessness burning the back of her eyes. Now was the time to ask her husband for the truth, to watch his face and see if she could detect his lies.

But he looked away. "I've been having nightmares for a while."

Kailani watched his Adam's apple move slowly in his throat, up and down, as if he were trying to swallow the dreams. She didn't know what to say; she wished she had paid closer attention to the pamphlets. She had seen nightmares listed as a symptom but couldn't remember if it indicated something serious.

"I dream about body parts," he continued abruptly, as if the words, the dreams, had escaped his throat and once they were loose in the night he couldn't stop them. "Christ. You can't believe how many times we had to clean up corpses or just parts of them, Kay. You just wouldn't believe it. Those fuckers left bodies all over the place, bodies of their own people, all bloated and tortured and tied up and shit. Once we found just a hand, a little hand from either a woman or a kid, on the side of the road. Still had on a tarnished pinkie ring." Then he took a deep breath and rolled away from her.

Goose bumps fluttered across Kailani's skin and she ran a hand down her arm, trying to rub them away. She waited until Manny's breathing evened out and then she put her arm around his sharp hip, trying not to cling too tightly, needing to feel the wholeness of him next to her, his heat and breath, his flesh and bone.

She never did bring it up; never again did either of them mention michelle.c.rand@us.army.mil. Even after the men had been home for a month and Manny had gained weight and grown out his hair long enough to have gotten reprimanded by his first sergeant for letting it touch his ears. Even after their block leave spent in Florida, at Disney World, and then a few days at the beach, where they managed to "surf": Kailani bringing Ana out on a rented boogie board and riding the waves back in with her shouting in delight. Even after Manny was promoted and Kailani, ignoring the advice from Finance, told him to buy himself a new truck.

One afternoon, Kailani and Cristina sipped coffee, watching the kids on the playground, and Cristina leaned forward to say, "Girl, have I got some gossip for you."

Kailani stretched her legs out in the sun and nodded at Ana, who was at the top of a slide, jumping up and down and shouting, "Mom!"

"What gossip?" she asked, kicking off her flip-flops and burying her toes in the sandbox, loving the feel of it even if it was clumped and damp. Javier was at her feet playing with a plastic shovel, alternately gnawing the handle and then banging on the flattened sand.

Cristina licked at the foam of her latte, clearly delighting in her news. "There's this private in supply; she was with the guys in Iraq. She some blond little *puta* that everybody been calling a home-wrecker. Every married *chica* got to watch out for their husbands 'cause this private, she only like married men—"

"Don't tell me," Kailani said softly.

Cristina blinked her thick lashes. "You got to know. You got to be aware."

Kailani carefully took a sip of her coffee. "Don't even tell me her name." She looked at her toes deep in the sand and thought of body parts, hands and feet separated from limbs, lives and identities lost, bits and pieces left behind and buried in Baghdad. Her husband had just spent a year of his life there, a year she would never know or understand. There were things he had seen and done that he could tell her about in the middle of the night, and there were things that he could not.

The year was over. He had returned to her. He was home.

Kailani imagined going back to Oahu, maybe when Manny retired. They would barbecue at the beach across from her mother's backyard, the breeze pushing the palm trees against the horizon. They would watch the waves come in, blue and limitless, the rhythm hiding the tumult underneath, and they would know how lucky they were to be there together, intact.

"But—"

"I said I don't want to know," Kailani said firmly, her voice suddenly too loud. Cristina sat back into the bench, her eyes wide and disappointed. Then Ana started waving wildly, her small hand arcing for her mother's undivided attention, and, as Kailani watched in silence, the child slipped safely down the slide.

THE LAST STAND

Specialist Kit Murphy entered Abrams Gym slowly, still getting used to the hop and swing of his crutches, the pressure under his armpits, and the jerking motion of his injured foot. Everyone was acting as if this was a normal welcome home ceremony—there were unit banners and flags on the wall as well as a DJ with a red, white, and blue cowboy hat yodeling nonsense into his microphone. But no one was fooled, not with the doctors standing around. Kit could spot medical corps even though they wore their camouflage uniforms: the medics watched the thirteen returning soldiers too closely in that impatient-doctor kind of way, like they were hoping someone would fall over and make their valuable presence worthwhile. And the waiting family members cheered daintily rather than that stomping, raucous, happy-to-be-alive way that crowds usually behaved, all of them trying to keep the horror of the moment to themselves, not sure what to expect or wish for, watching their wounded slowly making their way back to the land of the whole.

Kit wasn't sure what to expect or wish for either

as he scanned the crowd for Helena. He hadn't been able to get in touch with her for over a week; lately it was her mom, Linda, who cooed at Kit over the phone as if he were a colicky baby in the throes of a tantrum rather than a husband trying to have a word with his wife. On the bus ride from the airport, he had been dreading this moment of standing alone, of being selected to get a pity-hug from the too-dressed-up FRG leaders or too-dressed-down Red Cross volunteers who greeted the soldiers standing unloved amid the embraces. But behind the loose-necked gaggle of veterans waving their made-in-China American flags, he saw Helena's red hair, the lift of her chin, and the widening recognition in her eyes. Kit felt his cheeks blush hot with embarrassment; he kept his eyes on her hair and wouldn't look around, afraid another soldier would see how relieved he was to find someone waiting for him.

"I didn't know if you got word I was coming back," Kit said from the passenger seat of Helena's rental car. Two months ago his Humvee had been hit on Route Pluto, outside of Sadr City, surprised by a clever little Iranian bomb that had been hidden under the corpse of a skinny dog. Kit had immediately been evacuated to the Ibn Sina Hospital in the Green Zone, then helicoptered to Baghdad International Airport, then flown to the Landstuhl Regional Medical

Facility in Germany, though of course he couldn't remember any of that. The doctors in Germany let him call home when the concussion had healed enough for him to string words together. At first Helena wanted to know everything about his injury and they would talk until an orderly came into the room or Kit passed out with the phone pressed up against his ear. But when he got to D.C., to Walter Reed, when the surgeries didn't seem to be doing him any good and nothing was healing the way it was supposed to, when a month had passed and then six, seven, eight weeks, it was harder to get in touch with her.

"I left messages with a nurse; I think her name was Valencia," Helena said, eyes on the road. "Didn't she give them to you?"

Kit shrugged. He knew all the nurses and they had some pretty unusual names, but none of them were called Valencia. It was the nurses who alerted him that something might be wrong, the way they seemed overly excited when handing him one of Helena's phone messages that she had asked them to write down rather than being connected directly to Kit's room, even though he was wide awake in his bed and playing last generation's Nintendo: *Helena called but didn't want to wake you up! Helena hopes you are feeling better! Helena is so happy you are coming home!* Full of exclamation marks with overenthusiastic hearts at the bottom. He would crumple the pink slips into tiny balls of anger. On his flight from D.C., his section of the plane was dotted with fellow battered soldiers leaning forward with sweat on their foreheads, all of them wondering if their wives would be waiting, and if they were, how long they would stick around when they saw the burn scars, the casts, the missing bits and pieces that no amount of *Star Wars* metal limbs could make up for.

"I'm here, aren't I?" Helena asked softly, lifting her right hand from the steering wheel and placing it on his elbow, a pat really, but that touch was everything he needed. Kit took a deep breath and knew just being with Helena again meant he was home.

They pulled into a Padre's Motel parking lot just outside the main gate, a big sign advertising rates of $180 a week, breakfast and HBO included.

"I thought you were going to find an apartment?" he asked.

Helena shook her head. "I just got here last night."

When they opened the motel room door, Kit immediately noticed the twin beds. He looked at Helena, who sat down on the corner of one, bouncing on the edge of the mattress like a kid with an attention deficit disorder.

"I thought two beds would be best for your

foot," she said, her voice oddly loud and cheerful. "You know how I toss and turn. You wouldn't want me to roll over on your cast in the middle of the night!"

"Yeah, I would." He sat down on the other bed and stared. He had been away for more than a year, he had almost died, and his wife got a room with *two beds?*

Helena stood up, flipping that waterfall of strawberry blond hair over her shoulder the way she always did when she was nervous. She went into the small kitchenette and opened the fridge with a Vanna White motion of her arm, illuminating rows of bottled beer. "You've got to be starving! Let's have a drink and order pizza."

Kit took the bottle she handed him and twisted the cap off so hard it tore little ridges from the skin of his palm.

They watched TV, ate a pepperoni pie, and Kit tried to drink enough Coors to not feel anything at all, wishing for whiskey. Helena, talking nonstop, told him about his old friends at home: how John Roark got a senior in high school pregnant and they married on the due date; how Sunny Shay was making a fortune on her sex toy website but Father Mellon refused to give her communion at Sunday Mass; how Tim Lewski got yet another DUI as he drove home after refereeing a kids' soccer game. Kit didn't speak or even listen, just watched her thin hands as she spoke, the way they fluttered in the air like Fourth of July sparklers.

Helena had been pregnant when he deployed. A lot of wives had been, as if the soldiers started trying to procreate when they got their orders for Baghdad, tried to imprint themselves in a desperate scramble for immortality before ending up in the unknown. She claimed that she was showing when he left but her belly looked just as sweet to him as it always had, a little round, maybe, but he liked that, liked that her body was so soft compared to his. She lost the baby at the beginning of the second trimester, and by the time Kit got back for mid-tour leave, she seemed unfazed by the miscarriage and wouldn't give him any details. She made sure to take her birth control pills for the fourteen days that he was there, and she told him that she wanted to move home with her folks, to take classes at the community college, be near her high school friends and wait tables at the restaurant where she used to work, Grits to Gravy. Kit hadn't objected. He had even helped put all their stuff in storage. He liked the idea of her with her momma. But now he wondered if she had met someone else, a waiter from Grits, a manager at the local Kmart, even her smarmy high school volleyball coach, who always hugged her too long, someone who had stayed while Kit was gone.

When the pizza was finished and the beer bottles emptied, Helena went into the bathroom and came out in a baggy sweatshirt and sweat-pants, her face shiny-clean and her breath minty, gave him a chaste kiss on his cheek, climbed into her own bed, and clicked off her bedside light.

"Sweet dreams," she said lightly, and Kit said absolutely nothing in return.

He woke a few hours later, his foot throbbing with heat. He imagined the skin swelling around the stitches and narrow steel rods, blood and pus seeping out, sand still flecked around the edges of the wound, as if Iraq would not let him go. He wondered if he'd be able to find his bottle of Vicodin in his duffel, then remembered how the doctor said it was his last refill, from now on he'd have to make due with Tylenol, and he figured he'd better save it.

He glanced over at Helena. She was making that cooing sound she made when she was in a really deep sleep, her hair hanging off the pillow and catching the green light of the alarm clock. Two A.M.

When he was deployed, in his cot at night, in a tent with eleven other guys farting and snoring and jacking off around him, he would make lists in his head to help lull himself to sleep. At first it was the same lists other guys made and swapped while on guard duty or during a long patrol, all those empty, hot desert hours to fill, like listing the five best Steven Segal movies, or remembering the winners and losers of as many World Series as possible, or all the different sexual positions tried with different women. But the longer Kit was in Iraq, the more specific his lists became. Like *All the Things at Home I Never Thanked My Wife For,* which was his longest. The current absence of all the things on this list perfectly illuminated how much life sucked in Baghdad. Besides the obvious, like how Helena cooked him a hot meal every night rather than served him food from a bag that had waited in a warehouse for a year, then rode on a boat for a few months, then sat on a truck for a few weeks, then was picked over by a disgruntled staff sergeant who took all the decent meals and handed lowly Kit *Chicken, Chunked and Formed, with Grill Marks,* or *Beef Frankfurters* (more commonly referred to as *Five Fingers of Death*).

The things Kit listed in his head, such wonders of Helena's female ingenuity, were: how there was always toilet paper on the roll and a backup within reach, unlike being caught in the shitter at midnight only to realize that the roll of scratchy Chinese toilet paper at his feet had been sitting in a puddle of urine; the mirrors in the bathroom were never covered with catapulted floss gunk or tagged with wannabe army Latino gang slang; there was always something cold to drink (and not just that small swishable amount that guys left behind in the fridge because they were too lazy to throw the carton out); the sheets were fresh instead of oily with old sweat and crinkly with new sand; the towels were dry rather than rolled up and damply soaking his pillow; his socks were matched and paired like little heads of lettuce in his drawer rather than shoved, stiff with days of use, under his cot; there were clean clothes to choose from instead of a pile to sniff through, and those clean clothes smelled like American soap detergent instead of the cheap, astringent cologne that the local national cleaners doused the soldiers' clothes with when they were contracted to do the laundry.

That list could go on for hours, and often did. Of the twelve soldiers crammed into a tent that could comfortably sleep eight (though most of the other tents were jammed with eighteen, all asses and elbows, so no one in Kit's tent was complaining), there was always someone coming and going to guard duty or to take a piss or cursing under his breath in his headlamp as he read letters from home. The sun in Iraq rose at 3:30 A.M. The spiteful light would burst into the tent every time the door opened like a nuclear camera flash that singed the retinas of all the soldiers tossing in their cots. Kit would pull his sheet over his head and think of his list with such fervent desire that the semi-unconscious state of longing was almost as good as being asleep.

And now here she was, everything Kit wanted, the only person who could figure out how to make something good of his situation, and she was there in another bed, as far away as she had been before he stepped onto the plane. Kit tried to sit, feeling around on the bedside table for the TV remote. He either wanted to throw it at Helena's head, as hard as only a Lincoln High MVP pitcher could, or click on the TV. The impulse to remain a functioning part of society won. He turned the volume up, glancing at her every few minutes, wanting her to roll over and blink those eyes, wanting her to smile at him and ask him what was wrong so he could talk to her, so she could tell him that things between them were okay. But she slept on and Kit watched cheetahs hunting on PBS, the twist and somersault as they brought an antelope down and then tore it into bloody bits.

He tapped the remote against his cast, pretending he had an itch, but that didn't wake her either. Kit fell asleep as dawn started to filter through the gaps under the motel curtains. The light of the television flashed over both of them in their separate beds, unheeded like a lightning storm.

• • •

They went to a Waffle House for breakfast and Helena drove the rental car, Kit sullen and yawning in the passenger seat.

"We can get your truck out of storage today," she said brightly. He shrugged. He didn't think he'd be able to manipulate his boot enough to drive a stick shift, but he didn't want to say the words aloud.

Inside, he ordered too much food, then watched his wife as she added creamer and sugar to her coffee and would not meet his eyes.

My wife, he thought, and outrage struck his chest as forcefully as a wild baseball. "Who is it?" he let loose, angry at himself for being angry instead of trying to win her back.

She glanced up. "Who what?"

"There's someone else, right?"

She moved her hand to touch his wrist but he quickly lifted his own coffee cup to get out of reach, the black liquid scalding the inside of his mouth.

"There's no one," she whispered.

Kit looked down at his place mat. "Three weeks ago you were telling me that you would find an apartment, that you'd try to transfer your credits to a school in Texas, that you missed me—" He stopped, afraid his voice would crack.

"Look at me," she said, and this time she managed to put her hand on his. Kit lifted his face and took her in. She looked exactly the way she had when she graduated from Lincoln High two years ago, sturdy and confident the way a girl who got straight A's and played varsity volleyball since freshman year ought to look. She had always been plain, pale-skinned, with a few freckles on her cheeks, blue eyes so clear you could only see pupils, and a slight underbite that made her chin look stubborn and ready for a fight. Guys looked at her because of her long red hair and then they usually looked away. But when she smiled, her jaw clicked back into its rightful place and anyone who saw her smiling usually kept looking and had no choice but to smile back; she seemed so aware of the people she was with, she seemed to watch them like she could take their pulse with her silvery eyes.

"I love you," she said just as the waitress put down their sunny-side-up eggs and his side of sausage, bacon, and pancakes. When the waitress left Helena leaned forward again. "I love you but I don't think I can do this anymore. I want to be home. I like my college classes and I need to be near my family."

"I'll get out," he said, and it was the first time since he'd seen those two separate motel beds that he felt hope. "I'll work at the lumberyard; my stepbrother's always telling me he'll give me a job. I've got only six months left of my commitment. You can wait that long, can't you? You can stay at home, I don't care. I'll get out."

Helena pushed her fork across her plate, piercing a yoke and watching it bleed across her hash browns. "You can't get out until your foot is better," she said softly. "I've looked it up. You'd get awarded partial disability, about twenty-five percent of your salary, and what's that? Six grand? What could you do at the lumberyard with your foot like that? And we're more than three hours from the closest VA hospital—how would you go back and forth for physical training?"

Kit sat back in the booth. He had forgotten about his foot. "Then I'll stay in. But I won't deploy again." His voice picked up speed. "The army will have to give me some cushy office job. I'll only be working from eight A.M. to five P.M.; it will be like a regular civilian job. I'll be home for dinner every night. You can handle that."

"I'm happy now." Helena shook her head. "I don't want to come back here."

"Happy without me?" Kit wanted to throw up on all the food in front of him, the eggs getting cold and hard with a film of gray grease on top.

She took an envelope from her purse and a breath to steady herself. "I talked to a lawyer." Kit looked over his shoulder to see if he recognized any guys in the booths behind him.

"These are the papers for a legal separation. If we separate and don't divorce, you'll still get your housing allowance and extra marriage pay, but you can move into the barracks and save up. I'm making enough money of my own so you don't need to worry about me."

"You don't want to do this."

"I do," she whispered, as if deliberately echoing the words that had once tied them together. "Yes, I do."

The waitress boxed up all the food they couldn't eat even though Kit had told her not to, and he held the foam awkwardly balanced on his lap during the drive back to the motel.

Three months into the deployment, his buddy Blake had opened up a package from home and found divorce papers underneath a bag of melted M&M's. Blake almost choked on his lip of dip, then went on a tirade so long, obscene, and flecked with tobacco spittle that their platoon sergeant, Sergeant Schaeffer, told him to shut up or go talk to the chaplain. But Helena hadn't chosen the easy way out like that, hadn't told him this news in a letter or over the phone; she had flown out to Hood, been waiting, was sitting next to him still. Hell, the thing that always set Helena apart, from the cheerleaders or ponytailed softball players eager to sit with Kit in the back of the bus, was her kindness. How she volunteered at the animal shelter, spent her Thanksgivings at soup kitchens, waited at the curb at dawn to give Pepsis to the garbagemen. Would someone who voluntarily hosed dog feces out of kennels really leave her busted-up and Purple Hearted soldier husband just days after he returned?

Inside the motel room, Kit decided to change tactics. While Helena was washing her hands at the bathroom sink, he stepped up behind her and put his arms around her waist, nuzzling his chin in the back of her neck. He felt her body stiffen.

"I don't care if there was someone else," he whispered. "It doesn't matter. Things can go back to the way they used to be—"

She turned so quickly, slipping out of his arms, that he almost fell over.

"I told you there isn't anyone." She paced the narrow passage between the beds and the TV.

"Remember how good we had it?" he asked.

"Good?" She spun toward him, her hands on her hips. "You were always training late at the range and working weekends. Our apartment smelled like vomit and paint thinner from the last tenants. The neighbors had slasher films blasting all night. I was afraid to go outside by myself."

Kit was suddenly very tired. He leaned into the wet sink and tried to take pressure off his injured foot. He stared at his wife. For thirteen months he had dreamed of their home together, the meals she had waiting for him, the hot running water, the refrigerator always full, the steady air-conditioning, and the comfortable couch. Everything in hindsight had seemed like a delirious indulgence, just to have electricity at the end of every switch and lightbulb. He had forgotten that Helena hated that apartment on Trimmier Avenue, how she had to use a pair of pliers to get the dishwasher to work, how the shower leaked water from one end of the bathroom to the other, how she tried to get a dog-walking business going and failed.

"We'll find a nicer place," he said dully. He no longer wanted to have this conversation, he didn't want Helena's version of their life together to ruin the one he held in his mind.

She was pacing again. "I wish I was a better wife." She stopped and looked at his foot, her eyes translucent with tears. "I just want to go home and start all over again." Then, so quietly he almost didn't hear her, "Alone."

So he called up some of his single buddies, Crawford and Dupont.

"Who's up for a day of drinking?" he asked, and arranged for them to pick him up.

He left Helena sitting on her bed, her thin arms crossed over her chest.

"Don't you want to get your truck?" she

asked. "And your things out of storage? I wanted to get you set up. . . ."

But Kit ignored her, rifling through his duffel bag for that last bottle of Vicodin, swallowing three without any water, not caring that they got caught in his throat. And he didn't take his crutches as he slammed the motel room door behind him.

They went to The Last Stand Bar and Grill. Crawford and Dupont got the usual stares when they walked in together. Crawford wore the white button-up shirts and skinny ties favored by proselytizing Mormons, argued against evolution, and was hooked on comic books. Dupont had the word *Afrika* tattooed across his dark shoulders, boasted about the wartime rap videos he had put on YouTube, and got a manicure once a week. But Crawford, Dupont, and Kit had done basic training at the same time, managed to get sent to 1-7 Cav, then spent the deployment together in Iraq. They'd trained, bitched, slept, and pissed together for the past two and a half years: it was the equivalent of knowing each other for about a decade in the civilian world.

The Last Stand was a First Cavalry Division favorite and the walls were studded with memorabilia to prove it. There was a badly drawn poster of the doomed Custer, who had commanded the 7th Cav Regiment, and newspaper clippings about the raffles and fundraisers that the bar had hosted in order to send packages to the soldiers overseas. There were signs stolen from Fort Hood parking lots, photos of soldiers in Iraq standing with thumbs-up in front of Saddam's palace or pitted desert landscapes, and unit patches that the customers tore off their uniforms and traded in for free drinks. But for a Cavalry unit renowned for its long-ago horsemanship and now destined to ride nothing but tanks and Humvees, the shining glory of the bar was the mechanical bull in the corner. Cowboy hats or baseball caps of those who had fallen off hung above the metal animal, nailed to the ceiling in warning.

"Isn't that sweet little wife of yours here?" Dupont asked, buying a round of tequila shots and canned Miller Lite to start.

"She's a bitch," Kit replied, and reached for the small glass of tequila and the yellow oblivion it promised.

"To ditching bitches," Dupont toasted, and the three guys swallowed the tequila and slammed the shot glasses on the bar.

Kit had turned twenty-one in Iraq, his birthday spent guarding Assassins' Gate, one of the checkpoints of the Green Zone, and that day his buddies had toasted him with hot canteen water that tasted faintly of bleach. After the desert, after months of hospitals and strangers, sitting with Crawford and Dupont while drinking beer at a bar felt like the best thing in the world. And they wanted to hear about his foot, all the gory details of his surgeries, the pain he was in, and most of all how many Vicodin he had left and what their value might be in the barracks.

It was "Boom Boom" Dupont who had ripped Kit out of the Humvee after the IED went off, the IED that turned the entire undercarriage of his truck into a fiery wall that consumed the five men inside. Sergeant Schaeffer had been sitting next to Kit and caught most of the molten explosion. His body threw Kit against the side of the Humvee and somehow, miraculously, shielded him from the flame until Dupont, from the truck behind, grabbed Kit by the right arm and pulled him out. Kit had escaped with almost every single bone in his foot pulverized and burns on his face and hands.

Sergeant Schaeffer had not survived.

"To Sergeant Schaeffer," they toasted for round number three, four, and five. The sun was setting outside, the fluorescent lights in the bar starting to glow in the dusk, and a few bottle-blondes in cowboy hats and short denim skirts were two-stepping near the jukebox. Kit felt the floor shifting underneath him.

"Take it easy," Crawford said when Kit stumbled up to the bar to order another round.

They had called Crawford "Choirboy" in Iraq because he didn't curse, dip, smoke, or drink coffee. But Kit had once gotten a look in his buddy's TUF box and, under the layer of X-Men and Black Knight comics, the guy had the biggest collection of Jenna Jameson DVDs Kit had ever seen. Crawford continued, "We've had time to get our tolerance back. The first week I was home I would get drunk just twisting the cap off a bottle of Jack."

"I'm okay," Kit said, reaching for his wallet. He wanted to call the motel, to make sure Helena was still there, but he ordered tequila instead.

He looked over and saw Dupont, six-four and darker than the smoke-stained bar walls, undulating to the country music as if it were a ballad by Mariah Carey. The girls at the jukebox smoked their cigarettes and ignored him the way most girls living outside Fort Hood ignored guys with high and tight haircuts. But Dupont had the grace and nonchalance that women inevitably wanted to get close to, and the tallest girl couldn't help but start two-stepping next to his swaying hips. Then he made a motion toward the hibernating mechanical bull. The girls lifted their eyebrows and shrugged, then followed him over to where the hats forlornly covered the ceiling like the scalps of Custer and his massacred men.

Kit sniffed his shot, winced, and downed it. He thought of Helena's life at home. The business classes at community college, nights at the Go-Go Putt with the high school friends she had never strayed from, her boss, Mackey, who called her "my girl" and gave her grotesquely untalented figurines he carved out of walnut shells, her gossip-loving sister who could talk for hours and just had twins, even her mom, Linda, with her big huggable arms and freezer full of everyone's favorite ice cream. Kit hadn't realized the idea of home could pose such a danger. That it could steal Helena away from him so completely. Or that it could never be his own home again.

"Let's ride that bull," Kit said, the warmth of agave in his stomach almost quelling his nausea.

"Don't be a beef-wit." Crawford finished his beer and looked down at Kit's cast.

"Trust me, Choirboy, I don't feel a thing."

Kit watched Dupont and then the blondes, in quick succession, get tossed from the bull, each of them donating something to the sacrificial ceiling. The girls lost their cowboy hats. Dupont left his T-shirt dangling from a lightbulb and, stripped down to his wife-beater and the smudged Louisiana Tiger inked on his right shoulder, was suddenly thin and shy around the ladies.

Something's got to go right for me, Kit thought, assessing the headless, legless creature. When Kit was nine and his mother was splitting up with his second stepfather, he spent the summer in Winnemucca, Nevada, with his mom's folks. Every day his granddad would take him out to a cactus-laden field and put him bareback on a horse, a sullen old mare that would bite a hand rather than take the sugar. Before she got the chance to sink her teeth into Kit's thigh, his granddad would hit her hard on the rump and she would gallop as fast as those old legs let her. Kit would hold on to the matted mane, his heels tight in her belly, and it felt like flying. If he could ride that mare, he could ride this metal thing, and maybe it'd help him get lucky with the blond girl who flashed him her light blue panties when she did a somersault off the bull. That would show Helena.

The guy manning the mechanical bull looked at Kit's foot. "You sign the release form?"

Kit nodded and he let him through.

Kit got up on the contraption carefully, getting his good foot through the stirrup and pushing the toe of his cast into the other. He grabbed the horn in the center of the saddle and just to act jaunty he lifted his left hand up over his head, rodeo-style. He heard Crawford and Dupont cheer wildly, and even a hoot or two from the hatless blondes.

The bull started to move, slowly at first, letting Kit get the hang of it. It seemed easier the faster it went. And it was like his granddad's nag. He could almost hear her hooves against rock and dirt below, the wind in his ears, and that rhythm, that perfect, beautiful motion of being aligned with another creature, mindless with adrenaline and the pounding. God, he loved this, why didn't he ride more often? What could beat this feeling? Damn, he could do it, he would do it. Blue Panties was his.

Then the bull lurched and started moving in a new direction and the tenuous hold of his cast in the stirrup came loose. He felt himself pitching forward, and if he had been sober he would have tried to tuck and roll like he had learned in Airborne School, but instead he landed hard and the pain that shot up his left foot into his spine forced tears out of his eyes. He stayed like that, flat on his back, until both Crawford and Dupont came running over and helped him up, his leg dangling uselessly behind.

They had to carry him into the motel room. Helena opened the door, her eyes swollen with sleep or tears, wearing one of his army gray T-shirts over a pair of sweatpants.

They put him on his bed.

"You sure you don't want to go to the hospital?" Dupont asked for Helena's benefit, and

Kit shook his head. "Call us tomorrow, okay?"

Then they left, heads bowed, and Helena closed the door behind them.

"You smell like you'll have a headache tomorrow," she said, going to the kitchenette sink and pouring him a plastic cup of water.

Kit drank, and when she filled the cup again, he drank that, too.

"I was worried about you," she said.

Kit crushed the cup and tossed it at the wastebasket, missing. "Well, soon enough you won't need to worry, right?"

"I guess not." She turned off the light and he heard the springs of her bed creak. "Is your foot okay?"

"No." He wanted to say that it was never going to be okay, that he couldn't screw it up any more tonight than it already was. His eyes started to get used to the darkness and he could make out her outline by the alarm clock's light, how she sat at the edge of her bed.

Kit tried to arrange the pillows behind his head. He would have to wait until Helena fell asleep and then he could put on the TV. He knew, with the pain, he wouldn't be sleeping tonight.

"Let me do that," Helena whispered, and stood. He lifted himself up and she arranged the pillows under his shoulders, the army T-shirt brushing Kit's face, and he could smell her skin, the warm, new-kitten smell of it, her apricot shampoo and the vanilla drugstore perfume she liked to put on her wrists. He put his hand out, he couldn't help it, and touched the ends of her hair. She hesitated, hovering over him, and then he felt the bed shift and suddenly she was next to him, breathing on his throat in the dark.

"Is this my consolation prize?" Kit asked, feeling an electric surge of cruelty rush through him so strong his hands began to tingle. "You want to make yourself feel better by giving the cripple one last lay before you leave him?"

"You're not a cripple," she whispered, and put her lips on his.

Afterward, she rested her cheek against Kit's chest and he watched the small rise and fall of her head in time with his breath. He could hear a thick saturation in her throat that meant she was trying not to cry, and he tried to think of something to say, something that would stitch her to him forever.

"You haven't asked about the baby," she whispered.

He blinked. "I didn't think you wanted to talk about it."

She didn't reply for so long he was sure she had fallen asleep. "I never told you about the sonogram." She lifted her head and Kit could see her profile, her nose and her tough little chin. "I heard his heart, Kit, his wildly beating heart. So strong. I could see it on the screen, too, like a fist opening and closing. Three days later he was dead."

Kit played with her hair, running his fingers through its length, wondering what she was accusing him of. "I called as soon as I got the Red Cross message—"

"I know you did," she said, and Kit felt a drip of hot water on his bare skin. "I just can't get it out of my mind." She hesitated. "The sound of that heartbeat. I wish you had been there."

"Me too." Then, in the dark, he almost told her about Sergeant Schaeffer, how his body had pinned Kit down, his arms outstretched over him like some Old Testament angel. How he could smell Schaeffer burning and he thought it was his own flesh. How Kit had cried in that Humvee, hearing his friends screaming in the smoke, every intake of breath frying his throat and lungs, tongue and teeth. He had tried to pray but he couldn't, just cried like a child, helpless, until Dupont got him out.

But he couldn't tell her. And he couldn't tell her about his foot either—how he knew he was going to lose it, how he would become one of those guys people glance at with a jolt of pity, trying not to stare. He knew that when they fixed him up with a metal limb he would be out of the infantry, and he needed Helena to know that without her, without the army, he would have nothing.

Instead of speaking, Kit kissed the top of her head and played with her hair until she fell asleep against him. Exhausted, body aching, still half-drunk, Kit fell asleep, too.

He woke up when she opened the dusty motel blinds and let the sun into the room. When the light exploded across his retinas, he thought he was back in his tent in Baghdad, unhurt and whole, but when he put his hand over his eyes he felt every muscle of his body throb from a combination of being thrown by a bull and thrown by tequila, and he realized where he was.

Helena turned toward him, dressed in dark jeans and a tank top, her hands on her hips. "I should have made you drink more water."

Kit glanced around the room and saw her suitcase packed and ready on her unmade bed. He saw his crutches leaning against the far wall.

"Should I leave the rental car?" Helena continued quickly, checking under her bed. "I could take a cab. But the rental place is at the airport so it's really best if I drop it off now. Maybe one of your friends can drive you to the storage unit for your truck?"

Kit tried to sit and agony blossomed up his left foot. "You're not still leaving—"

"I got you a bagel and some Gatorade; that should help with the hangover."

"Helena, sit down. Talk to me." He had meant to tell her about the lists he used to make, how each one of them made him realize how much he needed her, and how could he go back to a life without her now that he had categorized everything that made life with her so good?

She reached for her suitcase. "I really have to go. Call my mom's house when you get your cell phone activated." She took a step toward the door. "The room is paid until tomorrow; I didn't know when you'd want to check out."

Kit leaned over the bedside table and used it to help him stand up, sucking in his breath. "Wait."

But the door was open and Helena stood in the shaft of bright light, looking at him over her shoulder, her hair lit up like flame, her hand still on the knob.

"We'll talk soon," she said, the click of cracked glass shimmering through her voice. "I promise."

Kit made a move toward the door, throwing himself at it, hoping something would catch him before he hit the ground, a bureau, a chair, anything that would get him out that door, anything that would get him near Helena so he could touch her again, kiss that freckle under her eye and put his arms around her and he would not let her go. But the door shut behind her and there was nothing for Kit to hold on to, nothing to break his fall, and as his knees buckled beneath him he knew with certainty that Helena, that everything, was gone.

LEAVE

Three A.M. and breaking into the house on Cheyenne Trail was even easier than Chief Warrant Officer Nick Cash thought it would be. There were no sounds from above, no lights throwing shadows, no floorboards whining, no water running or the snicker of late-night TV laugh tracks. The basement window, his point of entry, was open. The screws were rusted, but Nick had come prepared with his Gerber knife and WD-40; got the screws and the window out in five minutes flat. He stretched onto his stomach in the dew-wet grass and inched his legs through the opening, then pushed his torso backward until his toes grazed the cardboard boxes in the basement below, full of old shoes and college textbooks, which held his weight.

He had planned this mission the way the army would expect him to, the way only a soldier or a hunter or a neurotic could, considering every detail that ordinary people didn't even think about. He mapped out the route, calculating the minutes it would take for each task, considering the placement of streetlamps, the kind of vegetation in front, and how to avoid walking past houses with dogs. He figured out whether the moon would be new or full and what time the sprinkler system went off. He staged this as carefully as any other surveillance mission he had created and briefed to soldiers before.

Except this time the target was his own home.

He should have been relieved that he was inside, unseen, that all was going according to plan. But as he screwed the window back into place, he could feel his lungs clench with rage instead of adrenaline.

How many times had he warned his wife to lock the window? It didn't matter how often he told her about Richard Ramirez, the Night Stalker, who had gained access to his victims through open basement windows. Trish argued that the open window helped air out the basement. A theory that would have been sound if she actually closed the window every once in a while. Instead she left it open until a rare and thundering storm would remind her, then she'd jump up from the couch, run down the steps, and slam it shut after it had let in more water than a month of searing-weather-open-window-days could possibly dry.

Before he left for Iraq, Nick had wanted to install an alarm system but his wife said no.

"Christ, Trish," he had replied. "You can leave the windows and all the doors open while I am home to protect you. But what about when I'm gone?"

She glanced up at him from chopping tomatoes, narrowed her eyes in a way he hadn't seen before, and said flatly, "We've already survived two deployments. I think we can take care of ourselves."

Take care of this, Nick thought now, twisting the screw so violently that the knife slipped and almost split open his palm, the scrape of metal on metal squealing like an assaulted chalkboard. He hesitated, waiting for the neighbor's dog to start barking or a porch light to go on. Again nothing. Nick could be any lunatic loose in the night, close to his unprotected daughter in her room with the safari animals on her wall, close to his wife in their marital bed.

Trish should have listened to him.

This particular reconnaissance mission had started with a seemingly harmless e-mail. Six months ago, Nick had been deployed to an outlying suburb of Baghdad, in what his battalion commander jovially referred to as "a shitty little base in a shitty little town in a shitty little country." One of his buddies back in Killeen had offered to check on Trish every month or so, to make sure she didn't need anything hammered or lifted or drilled while Nick was away.

His friend wrote:

Stopped by to see Trish. Mark Rodell was there. Just thought you should know.

That was it. That hint, that whisper.

Mark Rodell.

Nick didn't know who the hell that was, but his friend seemed to think he should.

So he called Trish, standing in line at the FOB for an hour and a half for one of the three working pay phones that served over two hundred soldiers.

"Who's this Mark Rodell guy?" he asked as soon as Trish answered the phone.

There was a pause, then her voice, too calm and easy. Too ready. "He's the new gym teacher at Mountain Lion. I told you I wanted a willow tree, for the backyard? Well, he brought it over in his truck."

Nick could hear himself breathing out of his nose. "Is he married?"

"No. Nick, don't blow this out of proportion. He's just a pal. He helps all the teachers who have husbands away."

"I bet." His voice veered too loud so he coughed into his camouflaged shoulder to contain it, then continued in a hoarse whisper, "I bet he is a huge help to all you poor, neglected, stranded wives."

"He is. I don't like the tone of your voice."

Nick shut off the tone, shut his mouth and said nothing, waiting for more of an explanation, for anything, but his wife followed suit and said nothing as well. He could have told her that she was all he thought about during the long patrols or the even longer days at the base, that he had pictures of Trish and Ellie all around his cot so they were the first thing he saw every morning when he woke up and the last thing he saw at night when he shut off his light. He even had a sweat-stained photo of them tucked into his helmet that he would take out and show his interpreters, the local town council, or random Iraqis on the street, just to have an excuse to talk about his wife and child. But instead he said nothing until his time was nearly up, just listened to Trish breathe, knowing that she was winding and unwinding the old phone cord around her narrow fingers and getting angrier with each passing minute.

"How's Ellie?" he finally asked, his voice softening, deciding to salvage a minute or two.

"Damn it—I'm late. I have to get her from Texas Tumblers." And Trish hung up.

Nick pulled the phone away from his ear as if it had bitten him. He stared at it until the sergeant in charge of enforcing the fifteen-minute call limit walked over to him and pointedly glanced at his watch.

From then on, Nick could think of nothing but Mark Rodell. In the chow hall waiting for a serving of barbecue and bleached-looking green beans, in the Tactical Operations Center, or TOC, where he read reams of intelligence reports, in his weekly review of the latest surveillance video from the Predator Unmanned Aerial Vehicle, otherwise known as "predator porn."

He thought back over the last months of his deployment, to the days Trish forgot to send him one of her quirky e-mails or the nights when a babysitter answered Nick's call, and all of the strained phone conversations in between. She had told him she occasionally went for drinks with her fellow schoolteachers or to the monthly game nights hosted by other military spouses whose husbands were deployed. It had filled him with relief to think of Trish clinking martini glasses with bookish friends or, even better, playing Bunco! with wives wearing their husbands' unit T-shirts. But now he imagined his wife swishing her dark hair in a dimly lit bar, lip-glossed and bare-shouldered, meeting the eyes of a stranger.

Three weeks later, Nick started planning his return.

He woke at dawn, wide awake but disoriented, as if startled by a mortar attack. He had wedged himself behind a wall of old and crumbling cardboard boxes just in case Trish decided to come down and look for something. It seemed like a great idea at almost three in the morning, but now, with a hint of blue light touching the corners of the basement, he realized that his head and feet were sticking out on either end. The odd noise repeated itself above his head, and he pulled himself into a fetal position, holding his breath. It continued long enough for him to realize that it couldn't be human, and he gingerly got up on his hands and knees, careful not to topple the boxes, and rose to his feet.

He held his Gerber knife ready, expecting a rat, but instead found a cat, an ugly little thing, flecks of brown and orange smudged through its gray fur. It looked up at him, then turned back to its scratching and finally squatted and shat in the corner of a box full of Trish's old college history papers. Nick bit the inside of his cheek to stop himself from barking out a laugh, and reached in to pet its head. He could read its collar: "Anne Lisbeth." It tolerated his touch, then leaped out of the box and wove its way through the detritus of the basement and headed toward the stairs. Nick dropped back down, knocking his head against the cement wall.

Ellie had been asking for a pet for a year now, begging every time they spoke, flip-flopping between cat, dog, chimpanzee. Of course Trish had decided on a cat, not a dog that could watch over them, that could bark or rip out an intruder's jugular. A cat named after Hans Christian Andersen's "Anne Lisbeth": the tale of a mother who abandons her infant in order to become a wet nurse for a count. Her own neglected baby dies and the mother goes mad in the end, haunted by the unloved ghost of her son.

It was just like Ellie to name a cat something so freakishly morbid. She'd become fascinated with fairy tales during Nick's last deployment. And not the Disney fairy tales, oh no, not those wide-eyed, fat-lipped princesses mincing around and breaking out into song. Ellie had gone to spend a couple of weeks with her grandma in Boston two summers ago and came home with a collection of Hans Christian Andersen and illustrated *Grimm's Fairy Tales*. Nick would read them to her every night when he was home. They were full of strange cruelties he wanted to hide from his child: the way Cinderella's stepsisters cut off their own toes in order to fit into her glass slipper; the huntsman giving the queen the still-beating heart of a stag instead of Snow White's; the orphan girl so beguiled by her red shoes that she is cursed to dance in them until her legs are chopped off with an ax. Whenever he tried to skip or edit any of the ghoulish bits, Ellie corrected him, staring at him with her mother's huge and serious eyes, disappointed with his omission.

Then Nick heard the faraway tinkle of his wife's alarm playing the Bizet CD it always did. He hid behind his boxes, listening as she waited for two tracks, probably doing her morning yoga stretches, and then rose from the bed, the springs gasping. He felt his gut loosen a little when he realized that she was alone; no voices, muted laugher, or heavy steps followed his wife's tread into the kitchen. Her slippers scraped along the hardwood floors and headed directly to the coffee-maker. He could see her clearly: her hair held up in a messy ponytail on the top of her head so it didn't get in her eyes when she slept. One of her mother's old robes draped across her narrow shoulders. Sweatpants loose on her hips. A Brown University T-shirt tight across her breasts, which still looked damn good for a woman who breast-fed Ellie until she was two.

He suddenly wanted to walk up those basement stairs as easily as the cat. This was his home, she was his wife, his baby girl was still asleep in her pink-comfortered bed. He was a fool. Then he heard Trish back in the bedroom, probably rooting around for her sneakers, putting on her running shorts and a tank top that showed off her nicely sculpted shoulders, getting her body firm for Mark Rodell.

The coffee machine buzzed above and Nick reached for a warm Gatorade. No, he wasn't ready to go upstairs yet. He couldn't let himself break. He needed to listen, to find out, to know.

Nick quickly unpacked while Trish was out running. He had fourteen MREs jammed into his assault pack—one for every day. There were also a few shelves of dusty canned goods in the basement laundry room that he could eat: peaches, pineapple rings, kidney beans, tuna fish. He had a two-quart CamelBak of water and three large Gatorade bottles that he would drink and then use as a urinal when his wife was home, and that he could dump when she wasn't. He also had his sleeping bag liner, not too soft but at least it was something, a set of civilian clothes in case he needed to go out into the world like a normal person, and a backup set of black clothing in case he didn't.

It seemed like every little bit of training for the past seven years had led him to this moment, to hiding in his own basement, his intestines tight with fear in a way they had never been in Iraq. Every minute he had spent in Baghdad, sifting through lies, brought him back to this, to his home, his wife, the entirety of his life. While he organized his possessions against the basement's damp wall, he thought about the TOC, all those intelligence reports, how difficult it was to discern truth from exaggeration and ambiguity. He interviewed informers and interrogated suspects, watched the blinking eyes, twitching hands, the sweat on their foreheads, knowing that every word was suspect, each sentence could be loaded with mistruths, familial vengeance, jihadism, fear, self-preservation, and maybe, just maybe, innocence. It was difficult to determine if someone was one-hundred-percent guilty, but nearly impossible to find someone one-hundred-percent innocent.

When Nick showed up for an interrogation, his soldiers would say, "Here comes Chief Cash, we're about to hit the jackpot," or "With Chief Cash dealing, we're gonna win us some old-fashioned Texas Hold 'em." Nick ignored them; he wasn't any luckier than anyone else. But he did happen to be paired with an interpreter, Ibrahim, who used to be a Baghdad taxi driver and knew every street and shred of gossip in the city. They were a good team, Nick and Ibrahim, listening, waiting, knowing how to be patient and how to ask the right questions, and occasionally it led to something, like a dozen rocket launchers hidden in a hole under a mayor's refrigerator. But most of the time it led to nothing.

Nick understood the slippery nature of his task. Sources lied. Eyewitnesses missed crucial facts. Even the intel experts stateside regularly screwed up. So when his buddy offered to check on Trish more often, he told him no. Nor did Nick grill his wife about the details of her evenings out when they spoke on the phone, to search for cracks and split them open. Nick knew that his friend wouldn't be able to get at the truth no matter how many times he stopped by the house. And the thousands of miles of static and dropped calls separating Nick from Trish made it impossible for him to find out if she lied. There was only so much that could be gained from talking. He knew from experience that the only way to prove anything beyond a reasonable doubt was to get inside the suspect's house, to find the sniper rifle under the bed, the Iranian bomb-making electronics in a back shed, the sketches of the nearest U.S. military base in a hollow panel of the wall.

The only thing to do was to find out for himself. To go home in a way that didn't give Trish enough notice to hide the evidence.

To go home and catch her in the act.

Forty-seven minutes after her alarm had gone off, Trish returned from her run, the latch on the front door clicking shut. At the same instant, Nick heard his daughter wake up—heard her jump down off her bed and her bare feet slap along floors, heard the high-pitched screech of her voice, "Anne Lisbeth! Anne Lisbeth!"

Nick winced; that ugly cat did not look like the cuddling kind. Knowing Trish, they had gone to some "no-kill" shelter and deliberately found a cat that no sane person in the world would adopt. He imagined Ellie with scratches on her face and bite marks on her hands and Trish gingerly putting peroxide on the wounds rather than admit she couldn't rehabilitate a fey cat. It felt good to create this jittery resentment against his wife just when the sound of his child's footsteps was starting to make him yearn for her small arms around his neck.

"Mommy, where's Anne Lisbeth?" Ellie's voice screamed from the kitchen, probably a few feet away from Trish, who must be wiping sweat from her lean face, starting in on her second cup of coffee in order to put on a smile for her early morning whirling dervish. Nick was amazed he could hear her voice so clearly; he would have to be careful about every noise he made.

"Maybe she's in the basement," Trish replied. Nick quickly scanned the dim room and spotted Anne Lisbeth sitting on her haunches a few feet away, staring at him.

The cat lifted a paw and indifferently licked. Nick made as if he was going to kick it and it shot off, a blur of raccoon gray, bursting up the stairs, and he heard his daughter's shout of happiness.

When Nick's mid-tour leave came up at six months, he just didn't tell Trish. He said he wasn't coming home; he said a private's wife was having severe complications in her pregnancy and Nick gave his leave to him.

"There isn't some single soldier who could make the sacrifice instead?" Trish asked. Then, when Nick didn't say anything, "Fine, be the good guy. That's what I'll tell Ellie. You can't see your daddy because he's being the hero again." She didn't sound angry or even that upset, just giving him shit because lately she always gave him shit about something.

"Anything you want to tell me?" he asked calmly. "Anything at all?" He wasn't sure what he was getting at, if he was asking for a confession or a fight.

There was a long silence, as if Trish wasn't sure what he was getting at either, and then the predictable talk of Ellie: A's in the first grade, her most recent piano recital and the birthday party he had missed, all the milestones and transformations that had passed Nick by.

"She misses you," Trish said softly, as if she didn't want their daughter to hear. Nick imagined Ellie paging through her *Grimm's* in the living room, arching a thin eyebrow when her mother's voice dropped low, knowing the way all children do when their parents are talking about them. Nick waited for Trish to say that she missed him, too, but she hadn't said that in months.

Trish continued, "Last night, during prayers, she asked God to blow up the bad guys before they could blow you up."

Nick tried to laugh but instead closed his eyes and pressed his forehead against the hot metal of the pay phone and felt like all the gravity of the world was pulling on his rib cage.

"Kiss her for me," he whispered, and two hours later he was boarding a plane for home.

Nick, being Nick, had every step planned out. When he was sure, absolutely sure, that his wife wasn't cheating on him, he would leave the basement. He would wait until Ellie and Trish went to bed. Then he would jog the four miles to the Travelodge just off Indian Trail and get a room. He would take a really long shower, shave, brush his teeth, make sure there wasn't any dirt under his nails, eat a hot meal, get a few hours of sleep in a bed. First thing in the morning he would change into the uniform that was carefully folded in his assault pack. Then he'd call Trish, catch her before her run, and tell her he was on his way, that he had gotten leave after all at the last minute and had to jump on a plane, that he hadn't had a chance to contact her when they stopped over in Kuwait, but he was here at the Killeen Airport, he was home, he was about to get into a cab and he couldn't wait to see her and Ellie. He would say that he loved them, he was sorry, he was everything and anything he ought to be. Then he'd hang up, tell the cabdriver to stop at a florist, and Nick would buy a huge bouquet and whatever stuffed animals he could get his hands on.

However, he did not know what he would do if he found out that Trish was indeed cheating on him.

The scrape of the car keys, the corralling of Ellie out the door, time for first grade, time for Trish to go to work at that Montessori School in the ritzy neighboring town of Salado, finger painting to Mozart, prints of freaky Frida Kahlo with monkeys in her hair gazing down at the kids. Nick started to go up the stairs and then hesitated, sat down on the dim bottom step and waited. Then the front door opened again and he heard the click of Trish's shoes moving quickly from the hallway to the kitchen. Ellie must have decided she needed something—a juice box or an apple or maybe her favorite Maggie doll. Something forgotten, always something, and then Trish was gone. The old Volvo pulled out of the driveway and Nick tiptoed into the civilian world.

The first thing he did was walk into the kitchen and look out at the backyard.

Sure enough, there was a willow tree sitting right smack in the middle of the lawn. A frail, spindly spider sort of thing. But big enough that it wouldn't have fit in Trish's car. Nick took a deep breath. So at least part of Trish's story was true. That was a good liar's smoothest trick, to plant bits of reality into the subterfuge. It was the untold that Nick watched for. The slipup. The contradiction. The nervous hands touching a cheek, an ear, the smile or frown that seemed forced, the desire to change the subject. Such obvious signs.

The cat stepped in front of Nick, weaving between his legs as if deliberately trying to trip him.

"Shoo!" Nick stamped his foot and the cat hissed and ran.

He opened the fridge and stared at the shelves of plenty: a gallon of organic milk, a block of sharp cheddar cheese, fresh squeezed orange juice, and weirdly hourglass-shaped bottles of pomegranate juice. Nick hadn't seen such vividly colorful food for more than six months. He poured himself a cup of orange juice, careful not to take enough to be noticed. He did the same with the milk and savored it, full fat and fresh. Then a handful of blueberries, cherries, grapes. The garbage bag was new and empty so he put the cherry pits in his pocket. He shaved a few slices off the cheese with his Gerber knife and let it melt in his mouth.

Then he noticed the two bottles of white wine, both opened. His wife always drank red. Did that count as proof or had his wife just started drinking something new? Maybe she had a girlfriend over one night who had brought the wine, maybe they watched movies, painted their nails, told themselves how good their hair looked, or did whatever women did when their men were away.

He carefully washed and dried his glass, made sure everything was put back perfectly in the fridge, and left the kitchen.

He went directly to the master bedroom and stood in the doorway. He had picked out this furniture set of dark mahogany, choosing it because the headboard had a pillow of leather pegged into the wood with medieval-looking brass nails. Trish said it looked like the Inquisition but that was what Nick liked—the bed seemed like it was made for history, that it would be fixed in their lives forever.

The room was immaculate. No strange baseball caps or sneakers, no boxers or tightie-whities in the laundry basket, no new lingerie in Trish's top drawer. His relief hit him hard enough that he had to sit down on the mattress. It felt like it always did, the bed, the room, the house; it felt like it was *his*.

On his way back to the basement, he walked through the living room and, like the bedroom, it was the same, the family photos spaced nicely around the flat-screen TV, an abstract oil painting over the fireplace, a few charcoal sketches perfectly accenting the black leather sofa. He ran his hands along the cushions as if he could channel who had sat on the leather from its soft touch. They had fought over it. Trish had whined and whined, wanted an ugly stuffed corduroy couch with clawed feet like an old bathtub, but Nick had won. Now the leather leered at him, so soft, so sexy. He had wanted it because he imagined making love to Trish on the supple length and then somehow they never had, she was a bedroom-only kind of girl, but now he wondered if, like the white wine, she had developed new tastes.

There was a day at the forward operating base, a day like any other, the guys coming in from their latest mission empty-handed, unsure if not finding a cache of guns at the local imam's house was a good or bad thing. They were exhausted, hungry, the Humvee's AC busted again, and they knew they had missed DFAC's one hot meal of the day. They exited the Humvee, snapped off their forty pounds of Kevlar, took off their dusty Oakley sunglasses, and wiped the sweat from their eyes.

A private was sitting on a folding chair cleaning his rifle and drinking Wild Tiger, an Iraqi energy drink reputed to be laced with nicotine, the radio at his feet blasting Stephen Stills's "Love the One You're With." He was singing along, intent on the greasy insides of his gun.

Nick stood listening and thought of Trish's hips sashaying to the refrain, *When you can't be with the one you love, love the one you're with.* She grooved on all those long-haired seventies sounds, Bee Gees, Rod Stewart, Eagles, whipping out her old high school cassette tapes when feeling frisky.

Then Nick heard a hissed "Motherfucker." He glanced up in time to see Staff Sergeant Torres, one of the most laid-back guys he knew, walk straight over to the private and stomp the radio to smithereens.

The private leaned back in his chair to get away from flying bits of plastic. Nick and two other soldiers moved in close, ready to pull the men apart if Staff Sergeant Torres planned on smashing the private's face as well.

Instead Torres looked down at the shards under his boots. "I'll pay for that," he said, then turned and walked back to his tent.

None of the men looked at each other, as if refusing to acknowledge what they had witnessed. They knew there was only one thing that would make a guy snap like that, make him want to crush those words out of existence, and it didn't have a damn thing to do with life in Iraq.

By the time Trish and Ellie returned from school, Nick was firmly ensconced and almost comfortable with his setup. He had shoved some of

Ellie's discarded stuffed animals into an old pillowcase and propped it against the wall as a cushion for his back. He had dug through the boxes he could reach and found a few of his books. Maybe not his favorites, his *How to Eat Soup with a Knife, Personal Memoirs of Ulysses S. Grant,* and *Crime and Punishment* were still in his office upstairs, but here were the books he had liked before he joined the army, his Grisham and Clancy and *Black Hawk Down.*

A couple of Ellie's fairy tales were here, too, a yard sale version of Hans Christian Andersen and a lesser known collection of Grimm. He picked the Grimm up gingerly, as if he were touching his daughter's hand. He wondered if she was finally over her obsession, if she was listening to ordinary stories now with happy endings, stories that other children liked, the fluff that made Disney worth millions. He opened it and started reading a story titled "Child in the Grave," whose first sentence stated: *It was a very sad day, and every heart in the house felt the deepest grief; for the youngest child, a boy of four years old, the joy and hope of his parents, was dead.* He closed the book and shut his eyes.

That was life. The motherless Hansel and Gretel, starving and lost in the forest, arriving at the cannibal witch's gingerbread cottage. The little mermaid rescuing her prince from the stormy sea, then giving up her voice and her fin for painful legs only to watch him fall in love with the woman he mistakenly thinks saved him from drowning. The young army corporal, a mere three days from going home to his wife and newborn, gets hit by a sniper. Such vicious twists dealt to the undeserving.

And those were the stories people knew about. The ones that stayed silent could be almost just as bad: the everyday horrors of lonely and quietly disappointed wives, of husbands deployed to the desert for years and years, missing their children's first steps, spelling bees, scraped knees.

Nick stretched; his neck and back ached from sleeping contorted on the hard cement. It was day three and he was starting to smell; as soon as his girls left for school he would risk a shower. And he desperately needed to dump the latest bottles of urine; even the cat shit above couldn't mask the acid and meaty stench of his slightly dehydrated, over-proteined piss. Trish hadn't been grocery shopping so he couldn't eat much of the dwindled-down fresh food but he could eat a can or two of tuna. She wouldn't miss a couple of tablespoons of mayo or slices of bread. Nick might even turn on the TV for an hour or two to see what was happening in the world.

So far there had been no sign of this Mark Rodell—maybe Trish had told him the truth,

Nick thought, letting himself feel hopeful. Maybe he really was just a pal.

Or maybe he planted the willow in the backyard and then planted something else. Nick took a deep breath and told himself he could live with that. He could forgive. He could handle it as long as Trish's feelings hadn't changed toward Nick, as long as she still loved him, and this . . . this *aberration* faded with time until it was nothing but a memory overshadowed by anniversaries and vacations and Ellie's high school graduation. He could do it, he could, if it meant keeping the life they had, the beautiful life of Trish next to him, her hip pressed against his in the night, her hands tracing the bones of his spine, her body pulling him toward her, against and inside her, to a place he knew and longed for, safe with her and home.

But what if, what if, damn it, the *what-ifs* burned his brain and he pushed his filthy hands against his eye sockets. What if it had happened in his bed, on his couch, in the newly redone tub of the master bathroom? Relax, he told himself, relax, don't kick the wall or kill the cat. Then he thought of the sergeant busting the radio to bits, how good it must have felt, that release and revenge, in crushing that sound into nothing.

That night Nick kept rearranging his pillowcase of Ellie's animals. It was after midnight and he couldn't sleep. His body missed his morning five-mile runs, missed the exhaustion of a long day of constant movement and thought, fueled by endorphins, adrenaline, caffeine. There was always another informer waiting with a story, the rumor of small arms crossing borders, or the sighting of a high-value target visiting a second cousin. There was always something for Nick to chase.

But now the only thing he could do was wait. He told himself that he needed a couple more days. He just had to get through the weekend and then he would be satisfied. If Trish lived blamelessly through a Friday, Saturday, and Sunday, then all was well.

He imagined her asleep above him, her brown hair fanned out across the pillows, her long legs kicking free of the sheets and twitching the way they did when she dreamed. Her bedside table set with the glass of water she filled each night but never drank, her wedding ring and pearl earrings in one of her grandmother's china teacups, the framed photo of Nick in uniform holding a confiscated AK, smiling as if he owned the whole damn world. He had seen that photo when he went into the bedroom, and what woman would bring a lover to bed if there was a picture of her husband with a gun staring down at them?

He rubbed his hand over his face. Trish had

been right. It was so damp down here that Nick felt like his skin was covered in a film of mold. Keeping the window open had actually made a huge difference. He reached out and touched the rough wall to his right. It was slightly concave and uneven, looked like something that had been crafted with a pickax. When they were first stationed at Hood four years ago, Nick had wanted to live on post, wanted Trish to be sur-rounded by other army wives and families. But she refused. She didn't like the exposed carports, chain-link fences, or the flat roofs of the houses on Wainwright, and at the time Nick was only a Warrant 1 and didn't have the rank to get assigned anything nicer. So they started looking off-post in Killeen and Harker Heights, looking at the housing developments that seemed to spring up overnight like mushrooms after a heavy rain.

Trish had chosen this particular house on Cheyenne Trail because of the basement; she said that it reminded her of her childhood and she couldn't imagine buying a home that didn't have roots deep underground. Nick had laughed at her, hoping she was kidding. They were in Texas, for goodness' sake, and basements were unheard of. But the original owner had also been the architect, builder, and contractor of the entire housing development, and he hailed from upstate New York and, East Coaster like Trish, he, too, had decided that he needed a basement. It must have cost him a fortune digging through that unyielding soil of rock and clay. A fortune for a whim. Which was also what Nick thought about the house. Sure, it was fairly spacious, three bedrooms with an office, wood floors, and ceiling fans. But they could have gotten a new house, unlived in, untouched, for less. But he loved Trish like that, loved her enough to do something crazy, loved her enough to buy her one of the only houses in Texas with a basement.

When he made it back from Iraq for good, he was going to rip out this moldering carpet and finally get rid of these damn boxes. Hell, they would redo the whole thing, make it a playroom for Ellie and her friends. Trish would paint huge murals on the walls and Nick would put up new shelving so that Ellie's toys didn't have to rest on the floor. Why hadn't he ever thought of that before? Trish in an old T-shirt with paint on her forehead, re-creating all those fairy tales in their gruesome wonder, and Nick would walk over and hold his bottle of beer to her lips. She would drink deeply, her eyes on his, and Nick would know there was no one else in her life, never was and never would be, and he'd find a way to never leave her alone again.

There were still no visitors by late Friday afternoon, day four of his precious leave, just his wife and daughter. Each day had been almost identical in its simplicity. His wife running every morning, his daughter rising and yelling for that hell cat, off to work and school, and then Nick would creep up the steps like some troll, elf, garden sprite, to steal food, wash his hands and face, peer at the photos of his family together and normal. He would retreat to his cave and his girls would come home, do schoolwork, eat dinner, get Ellie ready for bed, then Trish would watch TV and turn in early.

Tonight he could hear Trish singing softly while she made dinner, the fridge door opening and then sucking closed, the oven timer dinging, and Ellie singing along, not sure of the words but mimicking her mother. Nick fidgeted behind his wall of cardboard, desperate for Sunday to come. He cracked his knuckles gently, finally took out his flashlight, allotting himself an hour of its light to read a bit of the Grimm.

Then a sparkle of white gleamed briefly along the low basement ceiling—a car had pulled up in the driveway. Nick clicked off the flashlight, letting the book fall to the floor with a muted thud, his heart lifting in his chest like it wanted to crawl up and out his dry throat.

The doorbell didn't sound but Nick heard the unlocked door open and a man's voice push itself into the rhythms of his wife and child's song.

Nick fingered his Gerber knife and stood, ready to protect his family. But Trish's voice called back, comfortable and welcoming, and footsteps creaked toward the kitchen along the floor above.

Nick held on to his knife all through dinner, listening to another man tease his daughter, listening to another man chew and eat his wife's food, his weight shifting in the chair that Nick ought to be sitting in, opening beer bottles and quenching his thirst with all that Nick loved. He held the knife when Trish took Ellie to bed and he heard the interloper pace, heard him put some dishes away clumsily in the dishwasher, as if wanting Trish to hear him clean up, finally turning on the television set. Nick thought how easy it would be to walk up those steps and slit this stranger's throat and be out of the house and gone before his wife had finished telling Ellie a bedtime story. But he waited, waited because having a man over for dinner looked bad but it still wasn't proof.

Then Trish came down and her voice was low and she laughed a lot, softly though, as if shy to show her teeth, and Nick knew from the way the door of the fridge kept opening and closing and glasses were clinking that they were drinking those bottles of white wine. Then a stretch of silence that could only be a kiss, and Nick pushed the knife into his thumb until he bled, just enough to keep him angry instead of wanting to put it to his own neck.

• • •

Nick was still holding his knife two hours later when he crept up the cellar stairs, utilizing every ounce of stealth he had ever learned. He had his assault bag, all evidence of his arrival packed up and wiped clean from the basement, and could be on his way to Iraq by dawn. He kept thinking of the Little Mermaid. Hans Christian Andersen's Little Mermaid, not the singing movie desecration. How, brokenhearted, she went to the prince's room on his wedding night and looked down on his sleeping face, his arm thrown possessively across his new bride. If she killed the prince and his wife, she would be set free, back to the sea and the waves that could crash over her until all of this human awfulness had faded away and she was a soulless water creature again.

The moon was near full and filtered through the blinds of the windows, filling the house with a thick, underwater blue. Nick went into Ellie's bedroom and stood at the edge of her bed, close enough to touch her, close enough to see the rise and fall of her chest. She was curled around her Maggie doll, her hands cupped together by her chin, her lips turned in a faint grin. She slept like her mother—deeply, innocently, unafraid, dreaming things he would never know.

Anne Lisbeth followed him as he crossed the hallway, moving soundlessly from Ellie's room into the master bedroom, her eyes knowing and reflective green like a witch's familiar. Nick stopped at the threshold. There was his wife and there was a stranger sleeping next to her. Trish's face was tilted toward the door, a bare arm trailing off the bed, the toes of one pale foot poking out from the sheet, just as Nick had imagined her night after night. The man was turned away, his back a wall, his head half hidden by a pillow, anonymous. But Nick could see the ridges of his fragile spine and knew that he and his Gerber could take him. Easily.

Nick moved the knife from his right hand to his left and then back to his right again and took a step closer to the bed.

He had done it. Here it was, finally, after all his searching, after all the lies and lies and lies, the shifty informants with their misinformation and subtleties lost in translation. Here, in his own home, was a single and undeniable truth. Nick felt a wave of sweat seep through him and his bowels twist, but he felt a sense of relief, too, that finally, for once, there was no doubt.

The knife continued to move from hand to hand, the blade catching the moonlight, a pendulum swinging from one side to the next, a judge's gavel raised, and Nick waited to see where it would land.

YOU SURVIVED THE WAR, NOW SURVIVE THE HOMECOMING

Carla Wolenski spent the drive from Fort Hood to Austin, one hour and thirty-six minutes, leaning forward, hands gripping the steering wheel so tightly that she could feel her fingernails straining against her bitten cuticles. She was about to pick up her husband, the father of her child, from jail.

The collect call from the city correctional facility woke her early that morning. Ted hadn't told her why he was there, just asked her to come get him, and then they had been disconnected. Now, the long stretch of flat Texas highway before her, Carla imagined all of the things that could have happened the night before: drunken pranks gone wrong, jaywalking, urinating on a sidewalk, public intoxication, bar fights, car accidents, DUIs. Whatever it was, it was serious enough to warrant a night in prison, which meant it was serious enough that it could potentially ruin Ted's army career.

She turned off Guadalupe onto Tenth Street and saw the jail, an ordinary, concrete façade with narrow, parallel stripes of windows, looking more like a telephone company or municipal building than a place full of human beings forcibly removed from society.

Ted was sitting on a low wall in front, bent-shouldered under a DO NOT ENTER sign. He had gotten back from Iraq only three weeks ago, and Carla still felt a jolt of electricity flood through her whenever she saw him, a shiver of amazement that he was really home, a mental realignment that she had a husband living in the same time zone. She tucked her blond hair behind her ears and quickly pinched her cheeks to bring out the color; she wasn't quite used to him yet and, even in her confusion, tried to look like something he'd want to come home to.

Pulling up to the curb, she noticed that his khaki pants, which she had so meticulously ironed the night before, were rumpled with streaks of mud on the knees, the collar of his polo shirt hung open and askew across his shoulders, the buttons clearly torn off. He lifted his head, saw her car and stood, revealing a swollen cheek and a face smudged with grime. It looked as if some divine giant had taken a paper doll of her handsome husband, crushed it, then smoothed the remains onto the side of the street.

Ted got into the passenger side and put on his

seat belt, not meeting his wife's eyes. He did not speak, offered no apology, no gratitude, no explanation, just stared straight ahead.

"What happened?" Carla whispered, putting a hand on his knee.

"I don't remember." Still not looking at her, Ted covered his face with his hands, his knuckles misshapen and cut. He had taken command of Alpha Company at the tail end of the deployment. When Carla complained about him working too hard these past few weeks, he would point to the fridge, where he had stuck his job description under a magnet from the Waco Zoo: *The Company Commander of a Mechanized Infantry Unit is responsible for the health, welfare, physical fitness, training, discipline, and combat readiness of 130 soldiers. Responsible for the accountability and maintenance of vehicles and equipment, all assigned weapons, home station equipment, and deployment-provided equipment in the company, valued in excess of $50 million. Teaches, counsels, mentors, and develops all subordinates.* A night in prison could relieve him of this duty and there was no way to hide whatever he had done. Battalions on Hood received a monthly copy of all the police blotters in Central Texas, and if the blotter somehow didn't get to his command, a rumor surely would.

Ted put his hands out and looked at them, front and back, as if astonished to see bruises there. "I remember doing shots of Irish whiskey, then waking up with my face aching, in a cell that smelled like piss."

She thought he smelled like piss, too, and was glad she hadn't brought their seven-month-old baby, Mimi, along for the ride. "Is anyone pressing charges?" she asked. "Was it a bar fight?"

He dropped his hands on his lap but was careful not to touch her fingertips. "The cops said we were in the street. The other guy got away. That's all I know. And I'm done talking about it."

If he had just looked at her, put his hand on hers or, best of all, whispered, *I'm sorry,* she would have forgiven everything and anything. She would have said, *We'll get through this,* or *Your chain of command will understand.*

But he continued to stare into the distance and she felt her chest tighten around her own anger, around her own fear, and she lifted her hand from his lap. "What are you going to do?" She clicked on the car's blinker and pulled into traffic, emphasizing each "you" as if he were a stranger she had no responsibility for. "Do you have to go to court or pay any fines? Will you need a lawyer? Will they put a permanent letter of reprimand in your military file?"

Ted turned toward her, giving her that look of disgust he usually reserved for the times he happened upon Mimi nursing at one of her distended and blue-veined breasts, as if Carla were the intruder in the home, some marauding, grotesque creature with her leaking chest and baby-weighted thighs.

"Jesus, Carla, I said I don't want to talk about it. Can't you give me five friggin' minutes of peace?"

She shifted into third so quickly the car shuddered, on the verge of stalling out. "Peace?" All those weekends Ted had spent training on the range, the late nights preparing for Iraq, and the deployments themselves; all of those days and nights, months and years he spent excelling at his job, she had been home alone, making sacrifices as well. "You'll have plenty of peace since you've effectively destroyed your military career. But that's okay; it's not like you have a wife and daughter to provide for." As soon as the words left her mouth, she knew they were the cruelest things she could say.

"Fuck you," he answered.

Carla sat up so straight she almost hit her head on the window visor. She wanted to stomp the brakes and give him whiplash but there was an ice cream truck riding her bumper, singing its plaintive song.

She stared ahead, afraid that if she turned to look at her husband, she would burst into a volcano of furious, scalding tears. He crossed his arms over his chest as if he were slightly startled with himself as well, but also a little pleased. Carla rammed the clutch around the grid streets of Austin, then raced seventy-five miles an hour north on Highway 35 toward Fort Hood, hoping to force her husband to speak first, even if it was to tell her to slow down. But he only leaned the passenger seat as far back as possible and pretended to fall asleep.

Carla thought of college, of the night she had met Ted. She'd had a boyfriend at the time, a premed student with long, tapered hands and a Saab, but a few friends convinced her to put her books away and go to an ROTC frat party. She spotted Ted immediately, that square face and army-short black hair, T-shirt too tight around his biceps, jeans low on his hips, swigging from a bottle of tequila. He looked like everything she stayed away from in a boy. But he honed in on her, waltzing right over with that bottle of tequila and half a lemon, and he spent the rest of the night dragging her around like his personal shot glass, licking salt and lemon juice from the inside of her elbow, pulling her close and breathing fire down her mouth, and she swallowed every burning drop.

But right now, she wondered what her life would have been like if she had stayed in her dorm that night with her sociology textbooks and chamomile tea, if she had only gone to bed early and dreamed of being a doctor's wife.

• • •

They slowed down behind traffic outside the
Fort Hood main gate, near the big sign that
said WELCOME TO THE GREAT PLACE, FORT
HOOD. Carla always got a kick out of that opti-
mistic entry. Like everything in Texas, Fort
Hood's claim to greatness was an attempt to
seem bigger and better than—yet set apart from
—anything else in the country; a boast, a dare,
the flick of a huge middle finger at the rest of
the United States. But the sign in the opposite
direction, the sign that greeted cars as they drove
off the military installment, the sign she could
just barely read in her rearview mirror as she
slowed to a stop, seemed to Carla to negate the
grandiose welcome. It read: YOU SURVIVED
THE WAR, NOW SURVIVE THE HOMECOMING.
Under the words was a digital counter that
recorded the automobile fatalities of the soldiers
each month. It was always highest when a division returned from a deployment; today it read
16. As if that wasn't enough, resting on the
median below the sign was the twisted metal
skeleton of a car, so crushed and burned that
nothing made of flesh and bone could have
escaped its destruction.

It was their turn to roll up to the guard gate
when her phone began to ring. Ted lurched out
of his seat and said, "Don't answer that."

Carla hadn't intended to answer the phone until

her husband told her not to. It was illegal to talk on a cell phone while going through the checkpoint, and there was a seventy-dollar fine for talking on a phone while driving on post, but she clicked it open anyway.

"Can you hold on for a second? I'm going through the main gate," she said into the receiver. She heard a stranger's voice answer, "Yes, ma'am."

"Jesus, Carla." Ted stared incredulously. "All we need now is a ticket. The battalion commander will love that."

She put the phone in her lap, rolled down her window, and smiled innocently at the civilian guard who scanned their military IDs and the microchipped Fort Hood sticker on their car; he either didn't notice Carla's open cell phone or didn't care. However, the guard did look Ted and his tattered clothes over a couple of times before waving them through.

"Yes, hello?" Carla said into her phone, ignoring Ted, who crossed his thick arms over his chest so violently she was sure he must be hurting his bruised self.

"Hi, ma'am? You don't know me; I'm Leslie Gray. My husband is in, uh, your husband's company?"

"Leslie Gray?" Carla looked at Ted. He shook his head, then ran a dirty finger under his throat, telling Carla either to hang up the phone or that he was going to kill her, she couldn't be sure.

"This really isn't a good time—" Carla began. A military police car passed her on the left and Carla quickly put the phone to her right ear, hoping he hadn't seen her.

"Oh please!" the caller nearly shrieked into the phone. "Everyone keeps trying to get off the phone! I called the first sergeant, the platoon sergeant, even that nice born-again chaplain, and everyone said they can't do nothing!"

Carla's back stiffened with dread. The caller's voice was hoarse and blurry with tears, so frenzied that Carla missed her turn down Battalion Avenue. "Okay," she said into the phone. "But I only have a minute."

"Are you kidding me?" Ted shouted. "Then pull over and let me drive."

Carla pressed the phone against her chest and hissed at him, "What if one of your soldiers sees you on the side of the road? You look like a psychotic hobo." She put the phone back against her ear in time to catch a story, midstream, about Captain Morgan rum mixed with orange soda, an argument about whether Christina Aguilera was "hot," and then neighbors calling the military police. "I hit my husband first," Leslie wept in a voice that sounded Deep South and seventeen. "I pushed, bit, and punched at him until he finally hit me back. But I started it and I ain't pressing charges. And they're still making him live in the barracks instead of with me."

nursing bra, opened her eyes and pried the T-shirt free. She put her finger in Mimi's mouth and for a moment the baby was silenced, her hard gums with those slender-edged new teeth digging into Carla's pointer. The only sound in the room was a commercial for wart remover and Mimi's slurping. Then Mimi realized there wasn't any milk in this fingertip—*there was nothing in this fingertip!*—and started screaming again.

Ted's hands had dropped to his sides, his action-figure shoulders into a mortal man's slouch. He was looking at Carla, the white of his left eye filled with a starburst blood clot. It felt like the first time he had looked at her in a very long time.

He lifted his arms. "Do you want me to hold her?"

Carla glanced at Mimi, her gummy mouth open and gulping for air.

Ted said, "It's okay, let me try."

Carla watched him, unsure. Did he think she was mad at Mimi? That she was about to shake her baby when instead she wanted to shake him? It almost made her laugh, the sudden concern on his face. She stepped toward him and placed Mimi against his shoulder. He tried to pat the baby's back but slapped the back of her head instead, then readjusted, holding her tucked under an arm, facedown, like a football. Mimi screamed even louder.

Carla walked out of the room, then stood in the hallway and listened to the crying. She was almost glad Mimi's gasping sobs did not abate. Glad until her breasts, tortured by the cries, began to leak. She didn't have the energy to get out the pureed pears and carrots, bib and high chair, and let Mimi go Jackson Pollock on the white linoleum, but she also couldn't nurse in front of Ted after his "I will never touch those mammary glands again" looks of horror. So she defrosted some of her pumped milk, warmed it and put it in a bottle, taking her time while Mimi bleated away.

She brought the bottle into the living room. Ted was unsuccessfully tossing Mimi up in the air, which just made her cries bounce louder against the ceiling, only silenced when she landed in his arms and the air was momentarily knocked out of her.

"It's easier if you sit down to feed her," she said, handing him the bottle and then quickly crossing her arms over her T-shirt, hoping she hadn't leaked through the padding of her bra. Ted sat on the couch and inserted the bottle into Mimi's mouth. Her red lips seized it, the gums working, gnawing away at the pain of her hunger, and with a few wet gasps her cries were silenced.

Carla blinked, amazed, the way she was each and every time, at how easily Mimi's riotous fury

"That's unfortunate." Carla kept her voice as coolly professional as possible.

"Jimmy can't even visit me!" The voice at the other end of the phone was out of breath. "I waited a whole year for him—now he's only five miles away and he might as well be back in Iraq." Carla was struck with a sudden image of the girl: thin-hipped, mascara-stained, pacing a small apartment with dirty rugs and Plexiglas windows. Carla shook her head, trying to free herself of this vision of a life ragged with a different kind of war-torn.

Leslie exhaled and continued, "Everyone said that Captain Wolenski's real strict and he's the one who decided the punishment." Carla looked at her husband, nodding her head. "They also say Captain Wolenski could let Jimmy off if he wanted to. Please, ma'am, you'll talk to him, won't you?"

"My husband is just following army regulations for this sort of thing," Carla said, then heard the girl sob as if she would never be able to catch her breath again. "Wait, I didn't say I *wouldn't* talk to my husband. I just can't promise anything—"

"Damn it, Carla!" Ted shouted.

"Is that Captain Wolenski?" Leslie whispered. "Am I on speakerphone?"

"No, I'm in the car. That's some idiot on talk radio." Carla glared at Ted, who was shaking his head and staring out the window.

Leslie sounded like she had collapsed on the floor and was talking into the little exhaust fan at the bottom of a refrigerator. "Oh, okay. Phew." Carla heard the long inhale of someone smoking a cigarette down to the filter and she wondered how in the world the girl's lungs could carry on a conversation, sob hysterically, and smoke all at the same time. "I just thought a woman would understand, you know? I figured you might soften your husband up or something. Jimmy never raised a hand at me before, ever; he's the sweetest guy you'd ever know."

"Leslie, I have to go now," Carla said gently. "I'll speak to Ted, I really will."

"Thank you, ma'am." The girl's voice was quiet, as if she knew there was no hope of leniency but needed to talk to another human being, needed someone to listen to her cry, needed to blow smoke into a phone at a stranger just to know she was alive.

They pulled into their carport. Ted had already clicked off his seat belt and had his fist on the car handle before the car slowed to a stop.

"Her husband just got back from Iraq—" Carla started.

"You don't know what the hell you're talking about." Ted pulled the handle but didn't push the door open. "Private Jimmy Gray is six-four, two hundred and eighteen pounds, and his wife is five-one, wouldn't be a hundred pounds soaking wet. She spent the night in the hospital. Did she tell you that? Missing tooth, sprained wrists, bruised ribs? I have the photos and medical report upstairs; you can take a look."

Carla put her forehead against the steering wheel, feeling nauseated: Was she really defending a wife-beater?

But she turned her face toward Ted, glancing at his bloodied knuckles and the dirt on his pants before she looked him in the eyes. "Crazy things happen," she whispered.

He stared back. Stared as if Carla had taken her keys and used them to stab him in the testicles. *"This,"* he said hoarsely, flexing his empty, wounded hands, "is not the same thing." Then he got out, slamming the door so hard that the whole car shook.

Carla went to her neighbor's apartment to pick up Mimi.

"Thank God," Meg said, pacing her living room with a screaming Mimi thrown over her shoulder. "I don't know why she won't stop."

Carla reached for her daughter. "She is teething and seething," she said, kissing Mimi's wet cheek, which made Mimi take her small fists and smash them into her mother's face as hard as possible.

Carla knew that Mimi was hungry. In her haste

to get to the jail, she had forgotten to leave a bottle, and now the baby's exaggerated rage was springing from one insistent biological desire, the tears and beet face all symptoms of going without food for almost four hours. Carla hushed, rocked, and bounced Mimi on her hip as she walked toward home. "Shhhh, my little monkey-head," she said, cuddling the baby close. Mimi pressed her face into Carla's chest, trying to find her milk source the way a famished vampire bat with a heat sensor in its nose tries to find the throbbing vein of a cow. Carla had quickly nursed the baby that morning, latching her to a breast while sitting at the computer and printing out directions to the city correctional facility. Usually the morning feeding was the best part of Carla's day, having such stillness between mother and daughter, the shared joy and sustenance, Mimi's pupils reflecting Carla's face. Carla would feel an emptying out and refilling of quiet joy as she looked down at the sleep-creased cheeks of her daughter. She would think to herself, *This is happiness,* knowing at that small and tenuous moment she was everything her child needed. Except that morning she hadn't been able to let the world slip away, that morning she had been worried about her husband, worried about Mimi's future, worried because ever since Ted's return, it seemed as if something irreplaceable was about to break.

eyes moved slowly from mother to father and back again in a blissful state of half consciousness, utterly calm now and sustained. Ted smiled down at the baby and Carla could feel herself smiling, too, as she leaned closer, something tight inside of her coming loose. She didn't move her hand even though she could feel milk start to seep through her shirt, that internal heat spilling out into the open.

She thought suddenly of the Grays—Leslie alone and weeping, Jimmy in an anonymous barracks room—separated by an irrevocable act. She wondered if their every future caress, argument, and apology would contain the taint of that violence, would contain the realization of how easy it was to move from the ordinary to the unthinkable.

Carla kept her fingers steady on her husband's veined wrist, she kept the stillness between them, kept the televised news and the memories and the anger at bay for just a little while longer. She didn't know what would happen the following morning, month, or year, but, even if it lasted only as long as it took Mimi to finish her bottle, she and Ted were together. For this small moment, reflected in their child's eyes, they were happy.

GOLD STAR

Josie Schaeffer drove around the commissary parking lot looking for a space. She had forgotten it was payday. She *never* shopped on payday—when the biweekly paycheck was automatically deposited into every soldier's account in the United States Army at the same instant, and therefore into the checkbooks of the forty thousand soldiers' families here at Fort Hood. The parking lot was a tangle of women pushing overflowing shopping carts, kids hanging on to the back or skidding around in wheeled sneakers, pickup trucks with their beds weighed down with toilet paper and diapers.

Checking her watch again, she finally pulled into the empty Gold Star Family designated spot in front. She waited a moment, peering at herself in the mirror, composing her face into what she imagined an ordinary face looked like, tugging her mouth into a smile but then giving up. She knew the spouses walking by with their loaded carts were hesitating, trying not to stare into Josie's window, trading lifted eyebrows with the other women passing. As she got out and locked her car, a white-haired veteran paused by his truck in the Purple Heart Recipient space a few feet away. He was wearing a black baseball cap with VIETNAM embroidered in block letters across the front. He stepped across the yellow line between them, his ropey-veined hand outstretched.

"I'm grateful for your sacrifice," he said. "Our country can never thank you enough."

He made it sound as if she had willingly offered Eddie up; Josie shuddered but gave the man her hand. This is why she avoided the Gold Star spot: "Gold Star," with its imagery of schoolchildren receiving A's and stickers for a job well done, was the military euphemism for losing a soldier in combat. Family members received a few special privileges like this lousy parking space, but that meant the pity rising from the asphalt singed hotter than any Texas sun. Josie blinked to keep her eyes dry and the vet took a step back, seeing he had inflicted pain. "I'm sorry," he whispered.

Inside, the commissary was even more packed than the parking lot; shoppers inched their carts forward, each aisle a halting four-car pileup. Josie moved through the crush, keeping her oversized sunglasses on, hoping no one would recognize her. She glanced at the shelves and tried to remember how to feed a man. It was easier than she thought it would be—the items that her husband once craved stood out and she carefully filled her basket: a loaf of crusty French bread, a package of Swiss cheese, a wand of salami, half a pound of roast beef, a bag of tortilla chips, a jar of hot Tex-Mex salsa.

A soldier had called her about an hour ago, leaving a nervous, rambling message on her machine. "This is Specialist Murphy, ma'am. You don't know me but I was hoping I could come and see you sometime, if that's convenient with you. It's just, um, you see, I knew your husband." At that point Josie lifted her head from the couch. "Sergeant Schaeffer, your husband, well, I was with him the day the IED went off," the voice continued as she reached for the phone.

"Come over for lunch. Can you do that?" she asked abruptly.

"Ma'am? You mean today?"

Josie nodded into the phone, as if he could see her. "Today, as soon as you can."

"Um, okay—I mean, yes, ma'am. I'll be finished with my physical training at thirteen hundred hours. Is that all right?"

Josie looked around at the cluttered kitchen with its unwashed dishes, the stacks of news-papers and books covering her dining room table, the laundry she had washed the week before and piled up on her couch, still not folded. She had two hours before one o'clock and no food in the house.

"That would be fine," she said.

Back from the commissary with her groceries, Josie heaved all the rumpled clothes onto her bed and then did the same with the piled books and newspapers. She hesitated in front of the mirror over her bureau. Grief had disfigured her. There were bags under her eyes that never faded even when the crying finally did; her shoulders were curled into themselves as if she were trying to keep something fragile and cracked safe inside her ribs; and the weight she'd lost in the past three months had exacerbated the creases in her forehead and around her mouth. So aged at twenty-six. She brushed her bangs down over her eyebrows, pulled her dark hair into a pony-tail, and checked her T-shirt for stains. She couldn't remember if she had showered yester-day, but at least her hair wasn't greasy and her clothes seemed relatively clean.

In the first weeks after Eddie's death, there had been visitors, soldiers who came to her apartment and sat uncomfortably on the edge of her chairs. She almost hated the smooth-faced boys, each one of them alive, able to run their five-mile physical training at dawn, go to a Burger King drive-through, catch a movie, get picked up for a DUI. Able to do anything. They seemed to sense her blame, never accepting her offers of coffee or potato chips, afraid to look her in the eye, rarely speaking to her other than the army requisite "ma'am." But they stayed in her home for hours, waiting to be relieved by another soldier, as if acting on direct orders from their chain of command to keep guard. She knew they were there to ensure that she didn't starve to death or slit her wrists in the shower; they also ensured that she didn't stay in her bedroom with the covers over her head, weeping and compulsively remembering every moment of Eddie that she could. She had to exist because the soldiers sat on her couch and watched Fox News. They had known her husband, how disciplined and focused he was, and so she changed her clothes each day, vacuumed the rugs, wiped cola spills off the countertops.

There were also wives who timidly knocked on her door, first the CARE team led by the chaplain's wife, then wives from the FRG whom she recognized from past military balls and barbecues. But Josie had always kept herself apart, sure that she and Eddie would be out of the army soon and any military friendships would be a waste of time. The wives, too stunned to smile or speak, had stared at Josie, seeing their own worst nightmare. They made up for their silence with food, tons of it, exquisite meals or simple casseroles that Josie couldn't stomach, and they left bereavement cards on her table that Josie wouldn't read. She wanted to tell the women to go home and be kind to their husbands instead of wasting their time with her. *Take care of your man,* she would have liked to say, whispering, *Take care before it's too late.*

But the soldier coming over today was someone she wanted to meet. She wanted him to talk about her husband, to tell her a story so she could picture Eddie again, his wide mouth, his square fingers tapping his knee, his blond hair catching the sun as he tipped his head back in laughter. Already the Eddie in her mind was looking too much like the photos in the apartment, frozen and posed and still.

It was the moments in between that she was the most afraid of forgetting, the moments that were too ordinary for photographs, the small memories, like waking up with him in the morning, how he held his knife and fork when he ate dinner, the concentration in his blue eyes when he did a crossword puzzle, his feet propped up on the coffee table. Or the way he walked in after a week-long training exercise and sat down on the couch to take off his boots. She would climb up into his lap, put her arms around his neck, and press her face into his chest and stay there as he rubbed his stubbled chin over the back of her head. She could smell all the days he had been away in his uniform, the dirt from the field and the burned smokiness of his sweat, the thin smell of gasoline from his Humvee and the oil he used to clean his rifle. He would put his big hands around her back and she felt enclosed in his strength and knew he was hers again, at least for a little while. But now she had forgotten the texture of his uniform under her cheek, the sound of his boots slipping off his feet and hitting the floor, the feel of his fingertips on her back. She was losing him all over again.

"Hello, ma'am," the soldier said. He held a bouquet of carnations and his face didn't know whether to grin or look somber. "I'm Specialist Murphy. Kit Murphy, ma'am."

"Kit, please call me Josie," she said, opening the door farther, taking in the sight of him. He was young, twenty or twenty-one, tall and bony, his uniform loose around the shoulders and waist as if he had not always been so thin. His skin was the grayish white of a wet piece of paper and there were dark smudges under his eyes. It wasn't until he stepped across the threshold that she noticed his limp and peered at his left foot and the black ski-boot contraption. Then she realized who he was. Two months after Eddie's funeral, the army held a memorial service, awarding him the Bronze Star with the V for Valor, suddenly claiming he had saved someone's life. Josie didn't go. Eddie's father had flown down from Michigan to accept the decoration, taking it home with him. That was also around the time the soldiers stopped standing guard over Josie and the wives no longer brought food, as if the community had ascertained she was no longer a risk to herself. Without their vigilance, Josie started just stretching out on her couch all day.

"Are those for me?" she asked Kit.

He looked down at the flowers in his right hand as if they didn't belong to him, and his pale cheeks turned red, making him look almost healthy. "Yes, ma'am," he said. "I thought I should bring something . . ."

"They're very nice." Josie took the dangling bouquet from his hand. The smell of the flowers made her think of wet dirt thumping down on the coffin, black high heels that pinched her toes, and the Kleenex that disintegrated into pulp as she rubbed it against her eyes. She had tried to be a dignified widow but was barely able to breathe during "Taps."

Josie found a dusty vase in the kitchen and called out to the soldier, who still stood in her living room. "I hope you like roast beef?"

Kit nodded and walked toward her, pausing in front of all the frames. She had gone through their albums and removed her favorites, putting Eddie wherever she could—on the dining room table, the television set, nailed into the four walls—so that wherever she turned, he would be looking at her.

"Sergeant Schaeffer was the best noncommissioned officer I ever met," he said softly, picking up a photo of Eddie from his Ranger School graduation, forty pounds thinner than he'd been before Ranger School, his cheekbones sharp slabs.

Josie put a plate of sandwiches and a jug of instant iced tea on the table. Her hands were shaking and the tea sloshed against the rim.

"He loved his job, ma'am," Kit continued. "He made other people love their job, including me." He put down the photo and eased into a chair, sitting in front of the sandwiches and taking one before Josie had time to get out the napkins and plates. "He would say things like, 'There is an entire video game industry trying to copy what you men get paid to do every day,' or 'You defend your country, you carry a gun, you blow things up, what do you have to complain about, soldier?' " Kit laughed with his mouth full, his eyes on the photos ahead of him.

Josie poured sweet tea into a tall glass and slid it across the table. This wasn't what she wanted to hear. Eddie had been planning on submitting his exit paperwork when he got home from Baghdad. He could have gotten out of the army the previous year; his commitment was up five months before the deployment to Iraq, and Josie had been jubilant. But then he told her he couldn't leave his platoon right before they went to war—it was as if they had all been training for the state championships and now that the practice was over and the big game was here, he was abandoning them. "It's not a game," Josie had said. But Eddie didn't listen. It had been a fight that raged for days. She threatened to leave him, asked who was he really married to, damn it, her or his men?

That was why they had no kids—she wasn't going to have a child who only saw his daddy every other year. For the five years they'd been together she had used that argument against him, knowing eventually Eddie would want a kid more than he'd want the army, he would get out, and she would win. And then Eddie was dead a month before coming home to her, and there would never be a child now.

That was what her bargaining had got her.

"I want to hear about the IED," Josie said, sitting down across from Kit, balling up a napkin in her hands. "Nobody would tell me the details."

Kit swallowed his mouthful and took a huge gulp of his tea. Josie wondered when he had eaten last.

"He saved my life," Kit said softly, looking into his glass. There were crumbs on his chin.

"Did he *mean* to save your life?" Josie could feel her voice rise with that edge it had taken on lately when she spoke on the phone with Eddie's father, who seemed proud of his son for dying, for getting blown up thousands of miles from home on a roadside in the middle of nowhere, his blood soaking into another country's sand. "Did he know he was saving you?"

Kit moved uncomfortably in his chair and didn't look at her. "We were trapped in our Humvee and his body protected me from the flame, ma'am. It was almost like he was hugging me to keep me out of the fire."

"Almost like?"

Kit put his glass of tea down carefully. He kept his eyes on the table and blinked, sucking in his cheeks so that he looked even more starved and sickly. Then he lifted his face and his wet eyes finally looked into Josie's. "I don't mean any disrespect, ma'am, but does it matter? I'm alive because of your husband. He was the best soldier I knew and he saved my life."

She hesitated. There were so many arguments in her head, angry words to toss at this man in front of her, denials and recriminations. The first reports Josie had heard said her husband died instantly in the blast. No heroism, just death. But if Eddie had deliberately saved this boy's life, then he had deliberately sacrificed his own; he had been conscious and in agony, and he had known he was leaving her behind.

They sat for a while in silence, Josie holding her napkin, Kit with his hands on the table next to his half-eaten sandwich. He cleared his throat. "I would have been at the memorial service but

I was still in the hospital in Germany. I'm real sorry I missed that."

Josie shrugged. "I wasn't there either. The funeral was bad enough."

Kit nodded once, as if he understood pain was something you lived with as best you could.

"Thank you for lunch." He took a piece of paper out of a pocket on his sleeve and handed it to Josie. "Here's my cell phone number. Please call me if there's anything I can do. I'm pretty busted up but I can still take out the garbage and open jars of pasta sauce or whatever it is they say men do better than women." He tried to smile, a half smile that didn't touch his eyes.

"Wait," Josie said, standing. "Don't leave yet." She glanced around the kitchen. "I'll wrap these sandwiches so you can take them with you. I'll never eat all this food." But instead of getting out the tinfoil, she stepped around the table and stood in front of him, her thigh almost touching his bent knees. Kit looked up at her, alarmed, as if she might hit him or kick his wounded foot.

Before he could get out of his chair, she sat down in his lap.

"Ma'am, um, I have to be back at Head-quarters—"

"Shhhh," Josie whispered, linking her fingers around his neck. She pressed her face into the stiff folds of his uniform and felt the Velcro of his rank against her cheek. She tried to smell her husband, but this uniform was too clean, too new, this soldier too thin and fragile, so rigid in the chair, sucking in his breath. But Josie held on, the camouflage material swimming in front of her eyes, the back of his neck smooth.

After a dazed moment, Specialist Kit Murphy put his arms loosely around her and Josie Schaeffer clung to him, knowing this man was not her husband, that her husband was never coming back, but for now she was as close to him as she could get and she would not let him go.

AUTHOR'S NOTE

An army base in a time of war is a very insular place. The guards at the entrance gates check the cars and driver's licenses of everyone trying to enter, often turning people away if they don't have a special visitor's pass or military ID. And for those who live on base, they need never step foot into the civilian world—we have our own child care, grocery stores, gas stations, movie theaters, bowling alleys, libraries, and gyms, the demarcation line between Fort Hood and the civilian world beyond ringed clearly with a chain-link fence topped with barbed wire.

We have our own rules, too: grass that must be mowed before it reaches a certain height, roads that shut down completely so soldiers can run their length during morning physical training, times when the entire post comes to a stop and stands at attention to listen to the evening bugle rendition of "Retreat," parking spots for generals and sergeant majors or, more tragically, parking spots for families who have lost a soldier in combat.

In my stories, I tried to create a window into that world. I wanted to capture the moments that lead up to a deployment as well as those that follow a return. And I wanted to focus not only on the soldiers fighting on the front lines but also on the families that wait at home and try their best to stay intact, try their best to find everything they need within those guarded gates.

I began writing *You Know When the Men Are Gone* in Fort Hood, Texas, when my husband had just returned from his second deployment and was gearing up to deploy again. In 2006, soldiers deployed for a year or more, and spouses were grateful if their soldiers were home for an entire twelve months before heading back to the Middle East. So as much as I cherished having my husband safe and next to me, sharing a life together again, I was always aware of the fact that he was not going to be home for long.

These thoughts of a deployment color every aspect of a military spouse's life. When we meet another spouse for the first time, we ask, "How many times has your soldier deployed?" It is a way to compare years of experience in a few short sentences. It is our way, without the obvious map of a soldier's uniform, to check out the medals on the other spouse's chest, to know what she, too, has survived and what she is made of.

We make immediate friendships with other military spouses; we have no choice. The army usually moves a soldier and his family to a new base every six months to three years, depending was extinguished by a little bit of milk. She turned to leave. Just because Ted made Mimi stop crying once didn't mean anything. He didn't know what it felt like to have been sliced open in order to get the baby out, the ripping and stinging and healing that took too long, and then Mimi's all-consuming need for her every day and in the middle of the night until there was nothing left but the crooked sudden smiles and those eyes seeking Carla and only Carla. Ted had missed all of the baby's life. Carla just needed to pick her child up, walk out of the room, show Ted that she had had enough, that she was finally finished. She didn't want a man with memories that made him shout at a television set, flinch in his sleep, kick strollers, and now this battered cheek, swollen eye, prison urine stench. Mimi was her family now, not this stranger whose past year was nothing to Carla but fragmented e-mails and phone calls with a three-second delay of overlapping voices and too long silences, waiting for the other to speak, then both starting to speak at the same time. The hesitation and nervous laughter, the echoes of their own voices like ghosts of what they used to be.

"I never know what to do," Ted said quietly, as if he were talking to himself, as if he thought that Carla had already left the room. "Whenever I touch her, whenever I hold her, I'm afraid I'll break her."

Carla turned and looked down at her child's flushed face. Ted was holding the bottle crooked, angled too low, letting air bubbles into the baby's sucking mouth; there would be gas pains later.

She reached out and lifted his hand so that the milk would flow unhindered.

Ted glanced up. "Thank you, Carla."

The words surprised her, and she stood absolutely still, not moving her hand from his wrist. She didn't know if he was thanking her for picking him up at the jail, for being there when he got home from Iraq, for creating this baby in his arms, or for something as simple as moving the bottle.

"You're welcome," she said, staring at him. She could lift Mimi from his arms and breast-feed her properly, or she could remain like this, her fingertips on Ted's pulse, and suddenly it seemed as if this was the most important moment of her life, that either small gesture was larger than any decision she had ever made. Their fate depended on whether Carla walked out of the room with the baby or stood next to her husband. She bit her lip and wondered if this was the sum of a marriage: wordless recriminations or reconciliations, every breath either striving against or toward the other person, each second a decision to exert or abdicate the self.

"Hold it just like that," Carla whispered. Mimi's

on the soldier's job. This cycle of new neighborhoods, schools, zip codes, and time zones makes it hard for a spouse to work outside the home. We are far from our siblings and parents, cousins and childhood friends. The person we depend on the most in the world, the parent of our children, is suddenly seven thousand miles away and regularly getting shot at. So we create our own new and tenuous "families" with fellow spouses. The pizza play dates, informal coffees, and Family Readiness Group meetings—the structure they lend to our days, and the feeling that we spouses are in this together—help us get through the deployment.

While *You Know When the Men Are Gone* is a work of fiction, I hope that I was able to reflect the spectrum of the current army-family experience. There are so many more stories that I wished I had written; there are so many spouses who continue to inspire me with their constant support of their soldiers. They are independent, patient, fearless, remarkable men and women, and I am grateful to be a part of their community.

ACKNOWLEDGMENTS

I'd like to thank my amazing agent, Lorin Reese. Every time I told him the collection was finished, he would read it, then, in his no-nonsense Boston accent, tell me it was *not* finished, and I had better get back to work immediately. His suggestions made the stories infinitely stronger.

Thank you to my editor, Amy Einhorn, for being her legendary self, sharp-eyed, insightful, and kind. I wake up every day amazed and grateful to be working with her. Thank you, Marilyn Ducksworth, Stephanie Sorensen, Mih-Ho Cha, Kate Stark, and Michelle Malonzo for treating me like a superstar, and Ivan Held, Ellen Edwards, Halli Melnitsky, and everyone at Putnam and NAL for your enthusiasm. You have all made me feel that my stories are in the safest of hands.

Thanks to the people at literary magazines who printed my stories just when I started feeling like a lousy hack, especially Jenny Barber of *Salamander,* and Ashley Kaine, Betsy Beasley, and Robert Stewart of *New Letters*. And to my best writer/reader friends, Jenny Moore and

Olivia Boler, who scribbled things on my manuscript like "C'mon, does this really happen on an army base?!" Thank you to vastly talented authors Benjamin Percy and Jean Kwok, who are also generous with their time and knowledge.

Thank you to my family and friends, including my army "family" spread across the United States from Hawaii to New York. I can't imagine having made it through my husband's three long deployments without your wisdom and encouragement.

I'd like to thank my husband, KC, who is my first and last reader, my military expert, fact-checker, harshest critic and most adoring fan, who continues to brave my moods and give me honest criticism, and who makes every single thing I write so much better than I could on my own.

And finally, I offer my unending gratitude to my parents, Bobbie and Eamon J. Fallon, who have always supported me. They taught me to chase my dreams, and I have, and it's wonderful.

ABOUT THE AUTHOR

Siobhan Fallon lived at Fort Hood while her husband was deployed to Iraq for two tours of duty. She earned her MFA at the New School in New York City and lives with her family in the Middle East.

ADDITIONAL ACKNOWLEDGEMENTS
(continued from page 4)

Some of these stories have been published previously, in slightly different form: "The Last Stand" (as "Burning") appeared in *The Briar Cliff Review*, Spring 2008.

"Camp Liberty" (as "Getting Out") appeared in *Roanoke Review*, Summer 2008.

"Gold Star" (as "Sacrifice") appeared in *Salamander*, December 2008.

"You Know When the Men Are Gone" (as "Waiting") appeared in *Salamander*, May 2009.

"Inside the Break" appeared in *New Letters*, Spring 2010.

Excerpts from Book XXIII "The Trunk of the Olive Tree" from *The Odyssey* by Homer, translated by Robert Fitzgerald. Copyright © 1961, 1963 by Robert Fitzgerald. Copyright renewed 1989 by Benedict R. C. Fitzgerald, on behalf of the Fitzgerald children. Reprinted by permission of Farrar, Straus and Giroux, LLC.

Center Point Publishing
600 Brooks Road ● PO Box 1
Thorndike ME 04986-0001 USA

(207) 568-3717

US & Canada:
1 800 929-9108
www.centerpointlargeprint.com